BEFOR

The old man closed the door to his cottage. ⸺ creeping across the face of the moon. He tur⸺ willed his feet to move but they remained rooted.

'Come on, you have to do this,' he said through gritted teeth. He began to shuffle down the path, the chill combining with fear to increase his shivering. He hugged himself, rubbing his biceps with his gloved hands. The thick, winter coat he wore felt like tissue paper.

The garden gate hung askew but open, attached to the gatepost by a single screw. As he walked out onto the footpath it felt like he was wading through quicksand. The mist was thickening by the second as it often did – just another February night on the Dorset coast. His breath joined with the murk as he ambled up to the junction. He glanced up. The moon was being smothered; its usual brilliance dulled. It reminded the old man of a rusty, old penny.

'A devil's moon,' he said softly.

He reached the junction and turned towards the sea, wishing his friend were with him, although he understood why he wasn't – of course he did. He had a son to think of. No; this was his fight. He'd started it and now he must finish it – one way or another. He wondered if he'd see the mist disappear, the weak, late winter, morning sun's arthritic fingers tearing at it as if it was candy floss. He put the thought out of his mind.

He looked back towards the village, a place he'd called both home and prison for the past ten years. It was in total darkness. He wondered if any of the spineless bastards were watching him. He took his glove off and shoved his hand into his coat pocket. His fingers searched for the amulet but closed into an empty fist. He was just making sure he'd put it into a safe place, and not brought it with him. The confirmation was relief and disappointment in equal measure. Deep down, he knew, for this to work, he needed the amulet with him, but he also knew that if everything went to shit and it fell into the wrong hands, it was the end – the end of everything.

He reached the driveway, hoping his surveillance for the past two months hadn't been in vain. Unless something out of the ordinary had occurred, he should have the place to himself for at least an hour. He hoped that would be long enough.

The gravel crunched under his boots as he made his way up to the house, the ball of fear in his gut growing with every step. He wasn't afraid of dying. He'd had a long life, not particularly happy, but better than a lot. To keel over from a massive heart attack or die in his sleep in his own bed held no fear for him. What he was afraid of – was dying in this evil place.

He reached the front door, the oak, black and forbidding. He took a deep breath, turned the handle, and pushed. The door swung inward without a sound. He stood on the threshold taking more deep breaths, fighting the panic that wanted to force his legs to turn and run.

'You've come this far,' he said to himself. He stepped into the hall and listened. The house was silent, and he was sure they were over on that God forsaken rock. It didn't take long for his eyes to adjust to the blackness of the house as it was only marginally darker than the misty night.

He began to shuffle deeper into the building, not knowing the location of the final piece of the puzzle. He was sure if he'd brought the amulet it would have guided him. Suddenly, he felt like a fish out of water, lost and alone. The darkness closed in around him.

'You're an old fool,' he said, the panic increasing. He had never been a timid man, never one to turn the other cheek. Never afraid to fight his corner. However, alone in this house, he felt like a frightened child.

"Indeed, you are." The voice came from the gloom ahead, but the old man recognised the owner immediately.

"You're on the island."

"Yes, I am." A face emerged, hovering in the darkness, bodiless, grinning. "Did you really think a pathetic, old relic like you would be any threat? You should have taken a leaf out of your friend's book and kept your nose out." The face smiled. The old man knew it was all over. He cursed his stupidity as he heard the tiny, scuttling feet and felt the insects crawling over his boots and up inside his trousers. He started to cry, slapping at his legs. They were all over him. He could feel them biting, burrowing into his flesh. He lost his footing and fell, his hip slamming into the wooden floor, the joint snapping like a twig. He screamed in pain. Cockroaches and spiders of all sizes emerged from the collar of his coat and scurried into his open mouth and up his nose. He flapped his hands uselessly as his airway was blocked. His last thought before he died was one word – 'Sorry'.

CHANTER'S HIDE

BEN'S STORY

ONE

If I said I was sad when Uncle Ted died, I'd be lying. From what I remember of the old boy, he scowled at everyone and everything. Even my dad – his own brother – called him a miserable sod. Let's face it, when a relative you've only set eyes on a couple of times dies and leaves you a cottage in a coastal village in

Dorset, it's hard to feel anything resembling sorrow. Especially when it comes at a time when you're working your socks off wading your way through the slush pile of a leading publishing house, whilst trying produce your own magnum opus. Oh, and on top of that your wife's expecting your first child and she wants to give up her very well-paid job at a swiftly rising advertising agency to become a full-time mum.

Although I was looking forward to being a dad, the job situation was becoming a little depressing, to say the least, and to top it all I would be the sole winner of bread, the only person bringing home the bacon. I must admit, before the news of Ted's passing, I couldn't see any way that I could find any time, when my eyelids weren't trying to reacquaint themselves with each other, to devote to my own literary aspirations.

So, yes, when I was called to the reading of his will, expecting to be left a ferret or a collection of cigarette cards depicting steam engines or something similar, imagine my wonderful, mind blowing surprise when I became the proud owner of a cottage in the village of Chanter's Hide. Suddenly the future was looking much brighter. When I came home to Jan (that's my wife, by the way) and our town house on the outskirts of Knightsbridge (a place I was worried sick about being able to afford, after Jan gave up work) I was grinning so much my lips had stuck to my teeth.

"Don't tell me it was two ferrets," she said, a concerned expression crinkling her button nose.

I laughed and shook my head. "Not a ferret in sight."

She looked me up and down. "Well whatever it is, it must be small."

"Au contraire, mon amour," I said, the grin widening.

"You are becoming a little irritating now," Jan said. "Standing there grinning like an idiot. Spill before I feel the need to knee you in the nether regions."

"How do you fancy moving to Dorset?"

She scrutinised my face for a minute or so before asking. "Are you telling me your miserable uncle Ted has left you property?"

I nodded vigorously. "A cottage on the coast, can you believe it?"

She stared at me. "This is not funny."

I took her hands in mine. "I'm not joking sweetheart; we can sell this." I swung my arms around, indicating the albatross that was ready to hang itself around my neck. "Move to the coast with money in the bank and live life."

She sat down on a kitchen chair with a thump. "I don't believe it. Where is it?"

"A village called Chanter's Hide, not far from Bridport, apparently."

"That's where 'Morrison's' is. We used to call in most days when we stayed at West Bay."

"Mostly to top up on alcohol as I recall."

She smiled. "We got an occasional baguette."

I put my arm around her. "That was a lovely holiday – our first, if I'm not mistaken."

"It was, unless you count that wet weekend in Bridlington."

I shuddered. "I don't even want to think about that place. That cottage we stayed in should have been condemned."

Jan laughed. "It was bad, wasn't it? I'd never seen so much damp on one wall. Anyway, forget Bridlington, tell me more about Chanter's Hide. The name doesn't ring a bell. I remember Abbotsbury, where the swans were and that place where 'The Three Horseshoes' was."

"Burton Bradstock," I reminded her.

"That's the place." She sighed. "Oh Ben, I love it down there. I can't believe it."

"I almost believe there is a God, "I said.

"You heathen."

"This calls for a celebratory snifter."

"You're not going to sit there and drink when you know I can't – surely?"

I shook my head. "No, I shall remain standing. Don't worry, I'll get you a cranberry juice."

"You're a bastard, you know that, don't you? I could murder a glass of Chardonnay."

I opened the cupboard above the sink and took out a bottle Johnnie Walker Black Label and a whisky tumbler. I unscrewed the cap and splashed a general measure into the glass. I opened the fridge, took out the carton of cranberry juice and tipped some into squash glass, which I handed to Jan.

"Just use your imagination," I said, winking at her. I picked up the tumbler and held it out to her. "Cheers."

Reluctantly she tapped my glass with hers. "Cheers. I hope it chokes you."

I grinned. "Now that's not a nice thing to say to a husband who has just told his wife she is about to begin to live a stress-free life on the coast."

At the time, I didn't realise how far from the truth that statement would be. As I let the spirit burn its way down into my gullet, I felt at peace with myself. I was looking forward to the rest of my life. A life to be spent with the woman I loved, a child I would soon worship, in a cottage in a seaside haven. Let's face it – it was the stuff of dreams – or nightmares.

We put our house up for sale a couple of days later and were expecting it to be a month or two and a reduction or two in asking price before we managed to sell. Four days later, it sold – no offers and no quibbling. Even the estate agent was shocked. To top it all, the couple who bought it were first time buyers, so there was no chain. We could move to the coast and they could move into our old place. We were on a roll.

We both handed in our notices and, a month later, were looking forward to a new life.

So, there we were, in my beloved 1996 Range Rover, me driving, Jan navigating. We passed through Bridport and took the road to Abbotsbury. Just after passing the 'Three Horseshoes' pub and the garage in Burton Bradstock, Jan told me to take a left. I remember yelling – where? She said – there, you idiot.

I swung the wheel in the direction she indicated. I was starting to brake as the hedge loomed closer and then we were bumping our way down a rarely used track.

"Where did that come from," I said.

"It was there all the time," Jan said impatiently. "What's the matter with you?"

I shrugged. "Just tired, I guess."

That was the first time I felt slightly uncomfortable leaving 'the smoke' for the beautiful unknown. It wouldn't be the last.

We had travelled a couple of miles when the track graduated to country road status and about two hundred yards on, we hit a T junction. A signpost that had seen better days informed us that a right would take us to Dorchester whilst the left turn was unnamed. It looked as though there had been a sign at one point but all that remained now was a few aged splinters.

"I think we take a left," said Jan, a little uncertainty creeping into her voice.

"What does the map say?"

"I told you, it's not on the map. The solicitor said it was too small to be recognized by Ordnance Survey. I'm reading his directions, only by his writing, I think he missed his vocation, he should have been a doctor. Anyway, we don't want to go to Dorchester, so do a left."

I swung the wheel over and we carried on, hoping for the best. "I hope the removal van finds it all right," I said. "Anyway, what's this crap about Ordnance Survey not recognizing it. It's a village and it has a name. I mean they put bloody hills and all sorts of shit on their maps. I'm sure they don't have a 'Village Recognition Team' that decides which places go in and which don't. I mean, that's just ludicrous."

"I'm only telling you what the solicitor told me, Ben. And I don't know how Ordnance Survey works. Do I look like a cartographer?"

"Quite possibly, yes. I believe most of them are pretty normal, and I doubt any are as pretty as you." The old silver tongue never failed. Jan looked at me, sighed and punched me in the shoulder but the expression on her face was pure joy. I suppose I ought to introduce myself before we get any further. My name's Ben Ebbrell and Jan, as I have already mentioned, is my lovely wife. Anything else of relevance will probably find its way into this journal at the appropriate time. I'm not even sure why I decided to keep this diary. I've never been a diary person before but with this new life and the looming prospect of fatherhood, it seemed, somehow, the thing to do. I am a writer, even if unpublished so far, after all.

"Look." Jan pointed and, sure enough, the remnants of the previous road sign lay in the ditch at the side of the road, the DE of 'Chanter's Hide' all that was visible. It had, obviously, lain there for some time as the grass and briars had almost devoured it.

"It's not on the map, the sign might as well be non-existent. How do people find this place?"

We passed into the shade of massive, old oak trees as they met majestically, in a natural arch over the road, the sun's rays pin pricks through the density of their foliage. As the ancient trees released us back into the summer's sunlight, the first dwelling of Chanter's Hide came into view. A wide drive, liberally decorated with cow pats led up to ramshackle barns, where a muddy John Deere tractor was at rest. As we passed, I saw the farmhouse with its thatched roof and, who I assumed, was the farmer himself. He had a roll-up dangling from his lips. He waved then touched the brim of a peeked cap that was grubby with sweat and bird droppings. I waved back thinking, if the rest of the villagers are as welcoming as this chap, we'll get on famously.

We drove on, passing a rather pleasant looking hostelry named "The Duck and Pheasant", followed by a butcher's shop and a grocery. Thatched roofs were in abundance and I wondered if the village had its own thatcher. If it did, he would have to travel further afield for work as Chanter's Hide was a tiny village with a population of probably around seventy, at most. Apart from the main street, which led, eventually, to the sea, there were only two other roads, one of which housed our new home, 'Cooper's Cottage', a dwelling possibly owned years gone by the local barrel maker. That would explain the moniker. The road it was on was, imaginatively, called West Street, its opposite number not surprisingly, East Street. The main road was, indeed, Main Street.

We turned left onto 'our street' and fifty yards on parked outside 'Cooper's Cottage'. We got out of the car and surveyed our new home. A wooden gate, that had, at some point, been stained green hung askew, the top hinge hanging onto its mooring post by a lone screw. A privet hedge spread untidily from each side of the opening to meet its neighbours, both putting ours to shame. The front garden was small, about the size of four bath towels but what it lacked in length and width, it certainly made up for in height. To say it was overgrown would be an understatement, it was wild.

"Uncle Ted was no Percy Thrower, that's for sure." I said.

"Who's Percy Thrower?" asked Jan.

I shook my head. "You must have led a very sheltered childhood," I said. "He was a famous gardening expert. Used to be on the telly and radio. My Nan loved him."

"Your Nan? And you expect me to know him?"

"Well I do and I'm only a year older than you."

"That's because your Nan loved him. Obviously, neither of mine did."

I shrugged. "Whatever. It doesn't alter the fact that this poor little garden needs some overdue TLC."

"I'll leave that to you then, Percy. Come on, let's see if we can fight our way through the ivy and see what Uncle Ted thought to the inside of his house. If it's as bad as this, you've got a lot of work on your hands."

The ivy that covered the front of the building had, clearly, been left to its own devices since Ted's death and had started to claim the widows and front door. I took the envelope with the keys out of my jeans pocket, opened it and selected the large Chubb, marked 'front door'. I was expecting some jiggling and, maybe, a lot more juggling, trying to find the knack required to unlock this bright red portal. But no, the key went in smoothly, turned with no resistance and the door swung inwards, revealing the lounge. I think we both fell in love with the cottage there and then. The oak beams were as black as night and the walls a warm magnolia. A fireplace in the middle of the left-hand wall promised a cosy glow in the winter. It was just the feel of the place, it felt like home. I know that sounds like an overworked cliché but that was how it was. It was as if this house had been waiting for us.

"I love it," Jan said. "Charlie will too."

Charlie, by the way, is our unborn child. When asked if we'd like to know the sex of Jan's bump, we were both in agreement and declined the offer. Bump's name, however, was sorted. If she gave birth to a boy, we would name him

Charles, after my dad, who died from lung cancer when I was nineteen. There aren't many days when I don't think of him. My mother left the pair of us when I was only six years old to start a new life in Australia with a man called Sean O'Malley, previously my dad's best friend. Despite his devastation at this double betrayal, he held it all together. He continued to work at Barkers, building hydraulic cartridges, a job he'd had for two years and hated, to provide for the two of us. He'd drop me off at Auntie Carol's on his way to work, she would then take me to school, collect me afterwards and feed me. Dad loved his sister and the feeling was reciprocated. She loved me as well. She was a brilliant cook and spoilt me rotten. I don't have many memories of my mother and the ones I do are of a nasty, selfish woman who used to find pleasure in yelling at me. In all honesty I think that dad and I were better off without her. I don't remember enjoying weekends before she left but when it was just the two of us, dad and I had some really good times, bowling, fishing, having a kick about in the garden or just chilling, watching films or cartoons on the telly. As my dad didn't possess Auntie Carol's culinary skills, we'd normally eat pizza or burgers on Saturday night and join Carol and her husband, Tim for Sunday lunch. I loved my dad and still miss him. Although Jan never met him, she appreciates how much he meant to me. Mind you, if she hated the name, Charles, I feel there might have been some gentle but firm persuasion to urge me in a different direction. As it is, whether the bump is a boy or a girl, the little treasure will be connected by name to my Dad, Charles for a boy and Charlotte for a girl, both, obviously, addressed as Charlie.

So, there the three of us were, Jan and Charlie and I in the living room of our new home, a slight aroma of pipe tobacco still lingering. I put my arm around Jan and for a few seconds we were in our own, little world. The blast of the removal van's horn shattered our reverie. From the photos I'd been shown most of Uncle Ted's furniture was either dilapidated or so old it wouldn't have been out of place on the set of a remake of Oliver Twist, so, I'd had the cottage cleared to make room for our own stuff.

"Best go and see them, before they take our furniture and dump it in the sea," said Jan.

When you have a moment like that, it's hard to return to reality. Briefly it was as if my dad was there with us. I gave the old chap a nod and a wink and went back outside to see the movers. I just hoped everything would go in without having to take windows out.

The two removal blokes were just getting out of the van, rubbing their knees, and having difficulty straightening their backs. I figured they must have racked up getting on for 130 years between them and it seemed apparent that they weren't still doing this because they loved it.

For several hours, we assisted Tom and George, the removal men, humping our furniture and cardboard boxes into our new home. If we hadn't, I think they would have been puffing and panting until midnight. Jan opened the box marked 'Kitchen' about halfway through, found the kettle and cups and made a cuppa for us all. She had had the forethought to bring a foil pack of teabags, a little pot containing sugar and a tin of that dried milk stuff with her. Now most men are used to refreshments being available when they desire them and, thanks to women, they normally are. I have to admit, when Jan produced these items, it just seemed normal to me. It's only as I'm writing this down that I see how much we take them for granted, women, I mean, not teabags. There are certain things us men know we don't have to think about, unless, of course, we don't have a woman to think about them for us. We are the dreamers; they are the pragmatists.

The four of us sat on the tailgate of the removal van with a 'brew' in our grubby hands. Tom took a hefty swig and let out a satisfied sigh. I wondered if he had an asbestos mouth, as I was still blowing mine, the dried milk not doing anything to cool the tea. As if reading my mind or thinking what a wimp I was, he said, "When you've been at this game as long as we have and you've drunk as many brews as we have, you become sort of…immune to the heat. Maybe you build up some sort of tolerance, I don't know. All I know is that if it ain't steaming, it ain't gonna do the job. What say you George?"

George was a man of few words. He took a similar swig, belched, and nodded.

Thinking about it, George was a man of no words. Since their arrival I hadn't heard a peep out of him. He and Tom had been a duo for a number of years, that was clear. They knew what they were doing, and vocal communication wasn't necessary. They'd perfected the puffing, panting, back stretching and pained expressions. It was all part of the act, ensuring as much help in emptying the van as was possible. I had seen Tom look at Jan's bump with disdain. Pregnant women weren't much use in the removal trade. She was good for tea making though and as he took another mouthful, Tom winked at her and grinned. "Nice cuppa Missus," he said.

"I'm glad it meets your exacting standards," said Jan, with a tight smile.

Tom looked at George and they both shrugged. After tea break, I stepped up the pace, wanting it over and them gone. I don't think they had upped their pace since the 1980s, so I hefted the rest of the boxes in while they struggled with the bed.

As they were closing the tailgate, the job done, mostly by me, I saw, from the corner of my eye, a figure approaching. I turned and was face to face with, who I assumed to be, the local vicar. I think it was the dog collar that gave it away.

He held out his hand. "Welcome to Chanter's Hide, Mr Ebbrell."

I wiped my hand on my jeans and shook his, wondering how he knew my name.

"Thank you, Reverend………"

He waved a hand. "My name's Simon," he said with one of the whitest smiles I'd ever seen. "We're not big on formalities here. I know it's a terrible cliché but we're just one big, happy family, which is why I'm here."

"Right," I said, my look of confusion, obviously, evident.

"I'm the welcoming committee, so to speak."

I'd seen a few 'men of the cloth' in my thirty odd years on this planet and I'm not saying they were all ugly, but I'd never come across one so slender, so well-groomed, and so bloody handsome. His lustrous, grey hair was longer than I expected of a vicar and he bore more than a passing resemblance to George Clooney. He was also charismatic. I don't think I've ever used that word in real life before. His eyes were blue but darker, more like a stormy sky at sunset – if I could have described it any other way, believe me – I would have.

"We're not really religious," I explained, uncomfortable under his intense gaze.

He laughed and I couldn't help thinking how perfect that laugh was. I mean, there are so many people who annoy you when they let out a sound like a braying donkey or a gibbering chimp when they laugh. I'd never used charismatic before and I'd, certainly, never described anyone else's laugh as perfect. In fact, I'm sure I had never had such strong feelings after a first meeting before, with either sex. I'd like to say except for Jan but, if I did, I'd be lying again.

"Ah, Mrs Ebbrell,"

Jan had her rubber gloves on and was coming to collect the mugs. Her face lit up when she saw the vicar and I couldn't curb my jealousy. I had never been jealous before, knowing we were solid, but at this precise time, watching her bat her eyelashes at a vicar, for God's sake, I was experiencing feelings I'd never known.

"I'm here to welcome you and your husband to Chanter's Hide," he repeated with another pearly white, disarming smile.

"I was just telling the vicar, I mean Simon, that we weren't really religious, babe."

Jan looked at me as if I'd just fell to earth from another planet. I wasn't surprised. I'd never called her 'babe' – never, and I had no idea why that had suddenly changed.

Simon laughed that perfect laugh again. "God is in all of us Ben and so is Satan. Who you decide to buddy up with is down to you. I'm not here to preach, just to ask you to come and meet the rest of our big family at the pub tonight. Shall we say 7.30?"

"It's been a long day," I said with a tired grin.

"We'll be there. Simon – was it?"

"Yes Jan, Simon Drake, at your service." He flashed that smile again and I'm sure I saw Jan's knees tremble.

TWO

Once he'd taken his aging good looks away, I turned to Jan. "I don't know about you, but I'm knackered. The last thing I could do with tonight is hobnobbing with the locals. I thought we'd sling something in the microwave, I'd have a couple of beers, you'd have a glass of your alcohol-free wine and we'd hit the sack."

"So, you'd shun all our new neighbours, would you? Village life is quite different, people look out for each other, that's the way it works. If we don't go tonight, what sort of message do you think that sends out?"

I felt like a naughty kid, being told off by his mother and bowed my head and shuffled my feet. "I just thought we'd spend our first night in our new home together, alone," I said quietly.

Jan smiled, shook her head and put her arms around me. "So, there is a romantic in there somewhere, is there?"

"I don't know what you mean," I said, sticking out my bottom lip.

"During the years we've been together, how many times have you bought me flowers, how many times have you surprised me with a home cooked meal or a restaurant meal even - knowing your cooking prowess, or lack thereof?"

I was hurt, I don't mind admitting it. Okay, she was right, I wasn't the spontaneous sort, but I wasn't a Neanderthal either. I guess I was like loads of men - and that thought just confirmed what she had said. I did take her for granted. Was I becoming a male chauvinist?

"Don't worry," she said. "You're better than most and, if I'm honest, I think flowers are a waste of money. Mind you, if you suddenly gained Jamie Oliver's culinary skills, I wouldn't complain."

"I'll bring you breakfast in bed tomorrow, the works, the full English," I promised, wondering how long you fried an egg for, so it was edible and didn't give you salmonella. Maybe I'd scramble it in the microwave, be on the safe side.

"That, I'd like to see," Jan said, with a chuckle.

"I might even throw in orange juice and coffee," I added. "Not into the breakfast, obviously."

"I prefer tea at breakfast time," she informed me. "You should know that."

"'Course I do. I just thought you might fancy a change, that's all."

"I'm looking forward to it. Now come on, let's try and get these boxes into the rooms where they belong, get showers and get ready to meet the village people."

"Should I put on my red Indian costume?"

"Yeah, and I'll don my hard hat and toe-tectors."

We both laughed and went back to work, me humping the boxes and Jan directing the proceedings. By the time we had finished the first stage of moving in, I found I was looking forward to our trip to our local, I had a mouth like the bottom of a birdcage.

Hitting the shower was a little presumptuous, however. The waterworks in Chanter's Hide didn't appear to be up to Knightsbridge standards. There was a lot of knocking and wheezing before the water dribbled from the shower head. The flow fluctuated, sometimes a drizzle, sometimes a spit, the temperature alternating between lukewarm and tepid. In future more time would need to be allocated for this simple task.

At 7.25 we left the cottage, heading for the "Duck and Pheasant". Jan wore a black, satin smock over charcoal grey slacks and looked gorgeous. I, on the other hand, wore a pair of faded Levi's and my favourite 'Tom Waits' T shirt, depicting the 'Swordfishtrombones' album cover. Jan had, long ago, stopped trying to influence my wardrobe choices. I'm a firm believer in individuality. I don't decry those who feel the need to conform. If that's what floats their boat, so be it. Don't get me wrong, I have always observed correct dress protocol at work but in my own time I reserve the right to dress how I wish and sphericals to everybody else. If they don't like it, they know what they can do.

The evening was calm, and the warmth of the day was still hanging on, the sun thinking about beginning its descent. I have to say I was feeling really chilled. A few beers before a well-deserved kip and then the rest of our lives ahead of us in this beautiful part of the world, I could already feel the inspiration bubbling up inside. I felt confident that recognition as a serious author was an achievable goal.

"Don't get drunk and make a fool of yourself." Jan's directive pulled me from my reverie.

"Me? Get drunk? I think you're confusing me with someone else, a previous boyfriend, maybe?"

"Stop being a smart-arse."

Truth be told, I have always had a penchant for the demon drink. Especially when I write, it seems to lubricate the gears within my creative engine. Too much, however results in literary compost. It's striking that happy medium, which, if I'm honest, doesn't happen that often. Before we left for Dorset, I'd already decided that my first published novel would be written without the aid of alcohol. The only thing that bothered me was that even with this bubbling inspiration, I was still struggling with the finer points. My head was an empty space, waiting to be filled by the coastal muse. Still there was plenty of time to think about that. Tonight, was about meeting the rest of the village, something I felt we'd been, more or less, ordered to do. I couldn't help wondering what would have happened if we had refused.

We turned onto Main Street and, as we strolled along, I looked at the cottages on my right, trying to imagine the sort of people who lived in each cottage, by the garden and what I could see through the windows. It's a game lots of us play - right? The next place we passed surprised me. All the others had beautifully maintained gardens and the paintwork was immaculate, both on the walls, doors, and window frames. This cottage was worse than ours, the garden a complete jungle, the paintwork flaking off, the curtains faded but clean. And this is coming from an untidy, do-it-some-one else sort. As I was staring, a little boy's face appeared at the window. He waved at me and smiled, but that smile never touched his eyes. They were the saddest eyes I had ever seen.

I waved back, looked away for a second, shuddering as if his misery had penetrated my bones. When I looked back, the boy was gone. A man stood in his place. He had a stern face, topped by a mop of grey hair and his eyes held something as well as sadness. It looked like pity. His considerable paunch tried to hide beneath a checked shirt. His age was difficult to guess, but by his face with its road map of lines and the colour of his hair, I would have put him in his sixties. He seemed rather old to be the boy's father. He stared at me and as I was about to look away, he shook his head and turned his back.

"You're not cold, are you?" Jan asked me. "You just shivered."

"Probably just somebody walking over my grave," I said with a smile.

"That's a stupid saying."

"Most of them are, but we still use them, don't we?"

"You do."

"Okay. I do." I was in no mood for arguments. A few pints of strong, Dorset ale at our new local was becoming more and more appealing by the second. Within a minute we were outside the pub. Jan took a mirror from her bag, checked whatever it is women check, tucked her hair back behind her ears, took a deep breath and said, "Right."

"You set?"

She nodded and I pushed open the door. We both gasped, the place was packed and across the top of the bar was a pretty professional looking banner with the slogan "Welcome Ben and Jan".

Simon Drake, now in civvies, jeans and a 'Dark Side of the Moon' T shirt was immediately in our faces, shaking my hand and putting his arm around Jan, ushering us into the pub. "We like to push the boat out a little when welcoming new members to our rather exclusive community," he informed us, with that infuriating George Clooney smile. "Kathy has done us proud once again." He waved a hand to the bar. It was covered with plates and dishes. There were sandwiches, vol-au-vents, sausage rolls, pork pie, crisps and nuts of all kinds, crudités and dips, cheese and pineapple, cocktail sausages. There were even large bowls of curry and chilli and something I couldn't identify.

"Plenty more where that came from," said a large bosomed woman behind the bar. I'm no authority on women's make-up, believe me, but hers looked as though it had been applied by a poorly trained plasterer. Her lipstick, the reddest red I'd ever seen had overrun the lips, in an effort to make her unusually thin mouth fuller. I wondered if she was married. I imagined her husband, if she was, to be a skinny, subservient sort. Just shows how wrong you can be.

"This is Joe, Kathy's significant other," continued sickening Simon. "He looks after all of the marvellous ales in this wonderful establishment."

Well, Geoff Capes came to mind. This bloke was huge, muscles on his muscles, as they say. When he smiled, it practically lit up the room.

"Welcome to Chanter's Hide folks," he said. "Come on, dig in. My Kathy's been hard at it all afternoon to produce this masterpiece."

"I second that," said Simon, laughing. "Get yourselves a drink, and your first plateful of Kathy's feast. Everything is on us tonight, so eat, drink and be merry."

"For tomorrow you may die." I completed the biblical amalgamation.

"I didn't think you were a religious man, Ben," said the George look-a-like. If you're getting the impression that I didn't like the man, you may be right.

"I'm not," I replied. "Just well read, I guess."

"Indeed." He paused and looked me up and down. I have to say I felt extremely uncomfortable under his scrutiny. Then his smile was out again. "Come on, have some refreshments and then I'll introduce you to your neighbours."

Everyone seemed eager to shake my hand and kiss Jan on the cheek.

THREE

We ate and drank, at least I did. Jan was drinking orange juice as any good mother-to-be should. Mind you she made the most of the old eating for two business, polishing off nearly half a plateful of mushroom vol-au-vents amongst other things. I had a few ham sandwiches and a sausage roll or two, but I really got stuck into the local brew. After a couple of pints, I felt pleasantly mellow, even Reverend Clooney wasn't irritating me as much. In fact, as we were introduced to the 'Hiders' as they liked to be called, I found some of them to be quite likeable. The chap who'd waved at us as we entered the village that morning was Sam Templeton, one of two farming 'Hiders'. He was a good, down to earth specimen with a quirky sense of humour. His face was, if possible, a cross between Rowan Atkinson's and Daniel Craig's. Well, in my opinion it was, and I wasn't drunk yet. We had a bit of a laugh about one thing or another, it turned out he was a bit of a Spike Milligan fan and had read 'Puckoon' ten times, one of my own personal favourites. The other farmer, however, was not so affable. His name was George Porter and was, pardon my French, a right miserable bastard. He must have been around sixty and made me feel like something he'd stepped in. Neither farmer appeared to have a wife in tow, and I didn't like to ask in case they'd lost the pair of them in some freak, farming accident. I was just backing away from Mr. Porter when Jan grabbed my arm and pulled me round to face a couple about our age. He had a mop of unruly, blond hair that was attempting to hide a pair of sharp, blue eyes, almost piercingly blue. He had one of those faces that is instantly likeable, with his crooked nose and lop-sided grin. I'm probably not describing him too well. He was quite handsome in a weird sort of way and what he lacked in looks he made up for in charm. His wife (as she turned out to be) was rather plain, not ugly – just plain. Her auburn hair hung lifelessly, framing her unremarkable features. Then she smiled and that smile transformed her.

"This is Nick and Hannah," Jan said enthusiastically, and then to them. "This is my other half, Ben. Hannah is nearly eight months pregnant, the same as me."

Hannah was so small and slight; I hadn't noticed the designer bump beneath her blue smock top.

"Pleased to meet you both," I said, allowing the smile that George Porter had scared away to return. "And congratulations."

"The same to you two, too," said Nick, laughing. "Looks like we're going to have to become responsible parents about the same time. Scary."

Although his tone was light, I thought I saw a strange look of fear flit like a shadow across his eyes. We all laughed, although mine was a little forced, I must admit.

"How long have you lived here in Chanter's Hide?" I asked Nick.

"All of our lives," he answered. "We were both born and raised as 'Hiders'."

In the past I had never considered myself to be a person who was easily irritated, being, in my opinion, one of the most patient people I know. Since arriving here though and becoming a – I can't say the word – it irritates me so much, my demeanour had changed. In fact, Nick's likeability score had plummeted after this simple, yet bloody annoying, description.

As the night wore on, we were introduced to more and more 'Hiders' and I introduced myself to a few more pints of 'Plummer's Best', a brew that was more local than I had realized. This village even had its own self-contained brewery, run by Joe and his brother, Ray, whose surname was, you've guessed it, Plummer. Old George introduced us but the only thing I remember is a large and very red proboscis. As I sipped, what was probably, my fifth pint of 'Best' it seemed to fill his face until I was chatting to a huge, red honker. I have a vague recollection of asking what his worst was like. I have no recollection, however, of his reply if, indeed, there was one. The rest of the night went by in a bit of a blur, I must confess. I have been inebriated more times than I like to remember. In fact, before I met Jan, I was no stranger to weekend benders with a few of my mates. What, I suppose, I'm saying is, I'm no stranger to the demon that is alcohol and, over the years, have built up a reasonable resistance. Which, to the layman, means it normally takes a lot to get me pissed. Yet here I was, after half a dozen pints, practically whistling Dixie.

By the time we left, I was receiving loads of pats on the back from 'Hiders', some rather more forceful than necessary and daggers from Jan. Even in my drunken state, I remember thinking – I'm pissed but she's even more pissed. For some reason this set me off giggling, and I couldn't stop, as we wended our way homeward. Once, out of earshot of the pub, she gave her feelings full vent and words I'd never heard tumble from her beautiful lips, flowed in an un-lady like torrent. I'd like to say that this brought me to my senses but, if I did, I'd be – you know. I'm ashamed to say, the more she ranted, the more I giggled. Even a battering from her handbag (I told you she was pissed) didn't halt my extraordinary hilarity. I think the line 'unrecognizable to myself' from Springsteen's 'Streets of Philadelphia' summed it up nicely. In all my days as a fully paid up 'piss-head', I had never felt so disconnected. It was like I was a voyeur to my own life, a comedy so hilarious, yet so serious. I was totally aware of Jan's raging anger but incapable of acknowledging it. I didn't want to keep laughing in her face, but I couldn't stop.

"You're an arse-hole," she hissed.

"I know," I managed between fits of uncontrollable laughter. "I.... I...m a b...a...stard."

It wasn't until we passed the badly maintained cottage where I had seen the boy with the sad smile earlier that this irrepressible and unwanted lunacy left me. He was there again. I glanced at my watch, it was 10.35 p.m. but even with the lateness of the hour and his age, I wasn't surprised. This time, there was no smile, just a dreadful pleading in those expressive, brown eyes. Plummer's false high was gone, and I was left with this overwhelming sadness. As I looked into those eyes, tears crept over my cheeks and an emptiness absorbed any alcohol induced well-being I'd previously felt.

"Oh, you're getting all maudlin now, are you?" Jan asked with a well-deserved sharpness.

"He's so sad," I said softly. "So very sad."

"Who? What are you wittering on about now? You know how much I hate it when you get pissed."

"Him." I pointed to the window but as I did so the boy shrank back into the house.

"Oh great, you're hallucinating now. How strong was that beer? I've seen you drink twice that amount and still remain in control of your faculties."

"There's something weird about this place," I said.

"The only weird thing is how they can brew beer that knocks a hardened drinker like you, on your arse. That's the only weird thing."

I've never been one for premonitions or omens or any of that sort of stuff but, at that moment, I was aware of a softening of my views. People in my past had used the expression – go with your gut – and I'd never had a clue what they were talking about. Any decision I made was based on facts and carefully thought about. It all came from the head. As we walked the rest of the way home, however, my gut, not my head, was telling me to be wary. I know it sounds melodramatic, but I can't explain it any other way. By the time I put the key into the lock of our new front door, I was as sober as a judge, as the expression goes. I dare say there are several Justices of the Peace that like a tipple. Not even five minutes ago I'd been giggling like a love-struck schoolgirl, yet here I was cool, calm, and collected but with this strange feeling, sort of like butterflies but worse, playing havoc with my usual pragmatism. Jan interrupted my thought process.

"I like it here, so don't mess it up for us. I mean, for God's sake, get a grip."

I left my gut to its own devices and returned to cohesive thought. "It's been a long day. I didn't have much to eat. I'm sorry if I embarrassed you, my sweet. If I offended anyone, I'll apologise tomorrow. Right now, I think I need sleep."

Jan sighed. "You can be irritating at times but if you weren't irritating me, some other poor girl would have to suffer you, I suppose. I will have to take consolation in the fact that I'm serving the greater good. Go to bed, I'll be up shortly. I'm going to have a cuppa; do you want one?"

I shook my head, pointed to the stairs, kissed her on the forehead and was off up the wooden hill, as my dad used to call it. As hard as I tried, I couldn't erase that boy's sad face from my mind. I was confused but convinced all was not as it seemed in Chanter's Hide. I slouched into the bedroom, got undressed and slipped beneath the duvet. As soon as my head was on the pillow, I was away with the fairies and I slept a long and dreamless sleep. Normally a light sleeper, I didn't even wake when Jan came to bed. I slept the sleep of the righteous.

The next morning, I awoke with – what felt like – the seven dwarves hammering away in my head. I couldn't remember the last time I'd suffered with a hangover; I just didn't get them. Normally I woke up feeling ravenous. This morning, however, breakfast was the last thing on my mind. I turned my head, winced, and squinted at the bedside clock. It was 9.53, I'd slept over ten hours. I sat up, swung my legs out of bed and winced again. Even my ribs ached. I felt like I'd gone ten rounds with Muhammad Ali. I went to the bathroom, peed, and splashed cold water over my face. It did nothing to alleviate the feeling of nausea or urge the dwarves to take a tea break. I went back to the bedroom, grabbed a pair of joggers and a T shirt, and made my way downstairs. Jan was in the kitchen, the radio on, singing softly to James Bay.

"Morning," I managed to croak.

She turned and laughed. "You look like shit."

"No need to sound so happy about it."

"You only had five or six pints, didn't you?"

I started to shake my head but thought better of it when 'Grumpy' chipped off a bit of my skull above my left eye. "I know, I don't get it either. No beer can be that strong. Anyway, did you see old farmer Sam throwing it down his neck. He must have had two to every one of mine and I bet he's not suffering this morning. I mean, I don't get hangovers, I just don't."

"Newsflash, sunshine. You've just started." She pointed to the cooker. "D'you want some breakfast?"

I opened the fridge took a slug of milk and nearly shook my head again. "Nah, I need to get some fresh air. I'm going to take a walk, see if the sea air helps."

"Do you want me to come with you. I've got some scones in the oven, they'll only be another ten minutes."

It's only when you're unable to shake your head without causing yourself severe pain that you realize how restrictive it is. "No, it's all right sweetheart. I need to go now. The smell of those scones is causing my stomach to do somersaults, and the thought of jam and cream is something else. I'll see you in a bit."

I left the house and, although the sun was high in the sky, there was a light breeze attempting to combat the mid-morning heat. I walked slowly through the gate and down to Main Street. I took a left away from the hostelry that had caused my present condition and then, for the first time that morning, I remembered the little boy in the cottage window.

"Good morning Ben, you look a little worse for wear, if you don't mind me saying."

One moment I was alone, the next I was facing that bloody Clooney smile again. It was as if he'd appeared out of thin air. I tried a smile but probably managed a sickly grimace. He was fast becoming like dog shit - everywhere. He was back in uniform, the dog collar as pristine as his complexion, the sun practically glinting on those whiter than white teeth.

"I guess I'm not used to the local brew," I said.

"No, it does have a bit more of a kick than what you're probably accustomed to. I have the occasional pint, but no more. I subscribe to the adage 'moderation in all things".

"Yeah, you're probably right. Anyway, see you soon."

I left him in the middle of the road. I really didn't like the man.

As I walked, the biliousness subsided, and the dwarves began to tire. The thought of Jan's scones started to make my stomach growl with hunger rather than churn with disgust. The sea air filled my lungs and the sun lifted my spirits. I know it sounds corny, but I really did feel at one with the world. Within the space of a few minutes I'd gone from the walking dead to a beacon of glowing optimism. I'd even forgotten Reverend George.

One thing I couldn't shake though, was that kid's face. The sea appeared, glistening majestically under a clear, blue sky and with it a clearer image. It was as if he was directly in front of me, those sad eyes, brown and wide. But I suddenly realised, the melancholy was only half of what I'd seen. He was reaching out, practically begging. But for what? He lived in one of the most picturesque parts of the country, in a beautiful, little village. It was summer, the sun was a ball of fire, the sea, a wide, blue wonder, the air pristine, the 'gulls' cry so comforting. Why was this kid so desperately miserable? Why did I feel as connected as I did? Once again, my feelings had flipped. I'd gone from feeling at one with the world to feeling totally confused. I was beginning to wonder if Chanter's Hide was really hiding something. I vowed to meet the kid behind the glass and find out why he seemed to be craving my attention. That was definitely in the top five of my to-do list.

My troubled thoughts had brought me to the beach. It was mainly shingle with scattered patches of sand but looking out towards Lyme Regis, across the rippling, blue water was, almost, magical. I plonked myself down on a convenient, weather-worn rock and tried to clear my mind and enjoy the view.

About half a mile or so out to sea was a small island and I wondered if I would be able to swim out to it. I used to be a reasonable swimmer. Although it wasn't huge, it was large enough to make it onto an Ordnance Survey, but then if the village itself didn't warrant a mention, why should this overgrown rock get in?

I don't think I was too concerned at that time but, when I look back, I should have been. I mean, it was as if the place didn't exist. But there we were, complete with annoying vicar, in a place that, obviously, did.

More and more, I felt I needed to chew the fat with the boy at the window. I'd been here less than a day and I was feeling, to be honest, like Columbo on speed.

I waved a hand to the newly found island; why, I have no idea. It's one of those things you do and then think - why did I do that. I tried to focus on Jan's scones as I retraced my steps.

When I pushed open the garden gate, I could hear Jan's dulcet tones, battling with Cher's on the old classic 'If I could Turn Back Time', Cher winning despite Jan's valiant and extremely robust performance. If she'd sung any louder, she'd have cracked the windows.

The smell of home baking was almost intoxicating, and my stomach complained audibly. It didn't quite compete with Jan and Cher, but it was a close second. As I closed the front door she came out of the kitchen, that's Jan, not Cher, her panda apron straining over our bump.

"Well, you look ten times better than when you left," she said. "The sea air must have magical powers."

"Yeah, the sun and sea are a mighty combination, a true panacea. I bumped into that slimy vicar on my way, there's something creepy about him. I don't like him."

Jan's expression changed and I knew she was about to tell me something I didn't want to hear. "Erm, maybe tonight will change your mind." The way her tone went up at the end of the sentence, I knew that the next thing she would say would really piss me off. I was right.

"He dropped by while you were out and invited us for dinner tonight. I said......we'd love to."

"Great."

"I don't know why you don't like him, he's a lovely man."

"You just can't see past the George Clooney looks," I said grumpily.

"He looks nothing like George Clooney, what are you talking about?"

"Are you saying he's not good looking?"

She laughed. "Oh no, he's a looker but, if you hadn't noticed, he's a vicar and I'm a married, very pregnant woman. You're not jealous, are you, Mr. Ebbrell?"

"Don't be silly," I said. "I'm going for a shower."

"Talking of showers, I don't suppose you can do anything to improve the flow?"

I held out my hands. "Have I turned into a plumber? We'll ask George tonight, if he's got the number of a good one."

"That's another thing. My phone isn't working – no signal. We don't appear to have any broadband either, but I suppose your uncle Ted wasn't technologically minded."

I took out my mobile and saw the 'no service' sign. "Mine's the same. As far as broadband is concerned, I'll have to see what other people have got here. I doubt if there's any fibre in the village. They probably don't even have land lines." I joked. I headed for the stairs. "I'll be as quick as the plumbing allows me to be."

"Try to come down in a better mood," Jan called after me.

As I climbed the stairs, I began to wonder if that was it. Maybe I was jealous. Let's face it, our local vicar had a face that may, or may not, resemble George Clooney's, he had a slim, athletic build and, as far as women were concerned, had more than his fair share of charisma. Add to that, the fact that Jan went all goggle-eyed whenever the bastard spoke to her. I guess I was jealous. Jealous of his near perfect looks but more jealous of the way Jan looked at him. I tried to remember if she'd ever looked at me that way. If she had, I couldn't recollect it.

I switched on the shower, dropped my clothes on the bathroom floor and stepped under the feeble spray. The pipes banged and wheezed like an arthritic robot. I returned my attention to the situation between my wife and the vicar.

I spent a good ten minutes under the drizzle and by the time I was towelling myself down, I'd managed to talk some sense into myself. I'd never been the jealous type and here I was getting hot under the collar about a vicar. I mean, a vicar, for God's sake. By the time I re-joined Jan in the kitchen and got stuck into scones, with jam and cream she'd popped to our local shop for, both produced here in Chanter's Hide, I was back to being a reasonable human being. I still wasn't looking forward to our dinner date, however.

FOUR

We spent the rest of the morning with the usual 'moving in' chores, Jan unpacking and cleaning, me, re-fixing the garden gate and trimming the hedge to a more reasonable height. By the time lunchtime arrived, we were both hot, sticky and in need of refreshment. Jan had bought a few basics from the local shop and knocked up some cheese and ham sandwiches, a few tomatoes, sticks of celery, a couple more of her scones and some nicely chilled orange juice. I say bought, what she'd actually done was promise my services as a labourer and general dogsbody. It seemed Chanter's Hide existed on a barter system.

"This is weird," I said. "It's not just me, is it?"

"I think it's rather quaint," Jan said.

"That's because you get the goods and I do the dirty work."

"Stop complaining. Ena only wants you to shift a few boxes about."

Jan shoved everything in a bag, and we took ourselves down to the beach, the sun high in the sky, the early morning breeze gone. It was a scorcher and by the time we sat on one of the sandier patches, our shirts were stuck to our bodies. The waves lapped gently, the occasional spider crab floating into shore and sunning itself. It was one of those moments in time when all the pieces of life's complicated puzzle fall into place. We sat in silence, munching on the best sandwiches I'd ever tasted. The occasion probably had something to do with it, but I think I can be sure when I say that I'd never tasted bread as good as 'Chanter's Hide's' own.

"You know, I wasn't sure about the move," Jan said, dabbing her brow with a serviette. "But I think Charlie's going to love it here."

"What about you?" I asked her.

"Oh, I loved it as soon as I saw the vicar."

I looked at her sharply and she burst out laughing. "You're so easy to wind up," she managed, between the giggles.

I shrugged, grinned, and nodded. "Yeah," I admitted, although I wasn't convinced, she was really joking. Jealousy, even if unfounded, can still eat away at a person. Her mention of 'Mr. Wonderful' brought back unpleasant thoughts of our impending dinner date. A whole evening in his presence filled me with dread, especially if Jan was going to be mooning over him all night and him, all charisma and film star good looks. The thought made me want to vomit.

"It's only one evening," Jan said, as if she could read my mind. "I really don't get why you dislike him so much. He's just a village vicar."

"I'm telling you, there's something not right about him, I don't know what, but there's definitely something. I've always been a good judge of character."

"Oh, sure you have. I suppose that's why you got all matey with that Jonah Reece and let him con you out of five hundred quid."

"We all make mistakes. Anyway, that was years ago," I said indignantly. "And he was a con man, making people like and trust him was a major part of his job description. This is different."

"Just go with an open mind and see how it goes. You never know, once you get into a conversation, you might find you've got a lot in common. From his T shirt last night, he likes Pink Floyd and you love Pink Floyd. That's a starting point."

I shrugged. "We'll see," I said, my opinion unchanged and unwavering.

We went back the cottage and Jan headed upstairs for a nap. I retrieved my iPod from the car and sat in the lounge with my headphones on. Jan's mention of

Pink Floyd earlier and my present mood found me clicking on to artists, selecting 'The Floyd' and my favourite album of theirs – The Wall, a dark and disturbing masterpiece composed mainly by Roger Waters. I played air guitar along with Dave Gilmour and imagined lobbing the bricks I kicked out of that imaginary wall at our local vicar. After about twenty minutes, my left hand dropped away from the fretboard and my right slowed its strumming as my eyes closed and Simon Drake goose-stepped ahead of a battalion of Gerald Scarfe's marching hammers. He suddenly stopped, glared at me, and yelled 'Hey you' in a Scottish accent. The hammers sniffed the air like wolves, left turned, their intentions clear. I was about to be trampled under the staves of hundreds of Nazi hammers. I turned and tried to run but my legs were swamp-bound in a syrupy gloop and the more I struggled, the less I moved. The hammers had no problem with the gloop as, Christ-like, they trudged across it. I started to scream as the syrup held me and my stiff-legged executioners drew nearer.

"For Christ's sake Ben." Jan's not so dulcet tones rescued me as the first of those cartoon destroyers was about to crush my skull. My headphones had slipped down, and Roger and the boys were in full flow. "You need to get better headphones, or, at least keep them on your head," said Jan, her irritation apparent. "You and Simon might like Pink Floyd, but Charlie and I aren't fans, especially when we're trying to sleep."

I switched off the iPod. "Sorry my sweet. In my struggle to get away from those bloody hammers my headphones must have become dislodged," I said with a sickly grin."

"Hammers?" She waved a hand and went off to the kitchen muttering, "I don't want to know."

She had decided to bake another batch of scones to take to the vicar and I thought I might venture into the jungle that passed for our back garden. It was little more than a handkerchief, about ten metres by six but, like the front, what it lacked in area, it more than made up for in height. Grass and weeds had been left to their own devices for ages, by the look of it. A narrow path made a vague appearance every now and then, leading to a dilapidated shed at the bottom of the garden. A huge sunflower towered above everything, surveying its kingdom. I waded through the foliage to see if this tired, wooden structure held any secrets. Maybe there was a lost Thomas Hardy manuscript, after all, he was from these parts.

The door was held shut by a rusty latch that took a bit of work to release. As I peered into the gloom, something darted over my left foot to freedom. I turned, just in time to see a huge rat disappear into the undergrowth. I have to say my heart rate increased a tad and I was glad Jan hadn't seen our guest. She'd have had a fit. I found an old cloth and wiped the grime from the inside of the window, to allow in a little more light. There were no ancient manuscripts, only a pile of rusty tools and a black, metal box. I tried to open it, but it was locked. I put it to one side to peruse later and picked up a scythe. On a shelf that was clinging to the shed wall by, practically faith alone, was a pumice stone. I took that and the scythe and returned to the garden, showing it my new acquisitions, my expression determined and threatening.

Even if I do say so myself, I made a fair bit of progress over the next hour and a half. The back garden was less a jungle and more a ravaged wasteland by the time I returned to the house. One step at a time.

Jan stopped applying her mascara, looked at me with disgust and wrinkled her nose. "You stink," was all she said.

"So, would you, if you'd been hacking your way through the Amazonian rain forest," I pointed out. "It's pissing hot out there, if you hadn't noticed."

"Shut up, get in the shower and get ready," she ordered, returning to the important job of 'putting her face on'. I saluted, headed for the stairs, and wondered how much effort it would take to 'put my face on'. The closer our dinner engagement got, the more peeved I became. Most people, I imagine, are not happy when their other half plans a cosy evening in the company of someone they dislike, especially when the host is charming, handsome and a bloody vicar. I believe I said the last two words out loud but, by that time, I was in the bathroom. For the second time that day I stuck myself under the drizzle that was masquerading as a shower and washed away my hard-earned sweat, muttering as I soaped myself. I don't know what it is about sticking yourself under jets of water (no matter how feeble) that changes your outlook. It seems to wash away a lot of the negativity and replace it with good, old common sense. Okay, so I didn't really want to spend my second night in Chanter's Hide in the company of some religious Lothario, but it was just two or three hours out of, what would hopefully be, a long and happy life. Why do we build things up to be more than they are? At times we are our own 'Marshall' stacks, amplifying the shit in our sad, little minds. The 'human race' is a good term. Unfortunately, there are millions more losers than winners.

As I towelled myself dry, I decided to stop being a spoilt kid and get with the programme – as they say in the States.

I dressed very smartly – for me, black trousers, and my best pale blue shirt. That's another thing. Why do we keep things for 'best'? I guess that is something passed onto us by our parents, like the difference between good and bad. It's a shame that a lot of kids today don't have things they keep for best and realize that life is precious – for us all. When I watch the news and I see thirteen-year-old girls committing murder, I despair. For Christ's sake, what is the world coming to.

I re-joined Jan in the lounge, and we were set to go.

"Behave yourself Ben, eh?"

I sighed. "What d'you think I'm going to do – grab him by the throat?"

"No, I don't. Just try and be nice. Okay?"

"I'll be niceness itself," I said, smiling serenely. "Let's do this. Got your scones?"

She held up a Tupperware container and we were off, Jan leading the way.

FIVE

It was about ten to seven when Jan opened the garden gate and, I must admit, I felt a certain pride as it swung shut behind me. I looked down and nodded – a job well done. The heat of the day had dissipated a tad and a tepid breeze murmured quietly; my overgrown privet tickled by its soft touch. Apparently, the vicar's house was located at the end of West Street and bore the moniker 'Chanter House'. What else?

"I thought vicars lived in vicarages," I said, as we came to the crossroads. "I mean, all the vicars I've known lived in vicarages."

"And just how many vicars have you known, Ben?"

Never having been a religious family, I couldn't recall a single 'Reverend'. "Well personally, not many," I admitted. "But it's a well-known fact. Vicars live in vicarages."

"And most of those vicars also have a church at their disposal, am I right?"

"Possibly," I said.

"Well Simon's house has to act as both, vicarage and church." She said it as if she was explaining to a child. Her tone and the fact that she always referred to him as 'Simon' put my back up straight away. I decided the best course of action was to stifle my annoyance and keep schtum.

Jan sighed. "You can sulk all night if that's what you want to do. I'm going to enjoy myself."

I stopped. "Maybe you should just go on your own," I said with a shrug, finding and embracing my inner child.

"Whatever." She walked on down West Street with that beautiful gait that only heavily pregnant women have, leaving me, hands on hips, like a petulant kid.

"I'm not sulking," I said and caught up with her, with little difficulty.

"Are you going to stop all this ridiculous, jealousy stuff?" She asked as I drew level.

"What jealousy stuff? I'm not jealous," I said with as much conviction as I could muster. "I don't like false, smarmy bastards, that's all."

"For Christ's sake, Ben. Will you get a grip?"

"We're here," I said flatly.

A dry-stone wall gave way to a wide, wooden gate, its stain glistening in the evening light. A grey, slate plaque etched with 'Chanter House' in silver appeared defiant in its confirmation. The gate swung silently inward and we crunched eastward up a gravel drive, canopied by ancient, oak trees. A minute later, the house itself came into view, a huge, grey, stone mansion, its windows elaborately leaded. The front door was a massive slab of polished ebony, as black as coal, a silver knocker reflecting the sun's weakening rays. Jan grabbed it and gave it the old three and two rap. Within seconds we were face to face with one of the most beautiful women I'd ever seen.

"Good evening Ben, good evening Jan, I'm Shona, Simon's housekeeper. Please come in," she actually purred. I never thought I'd ever use that word to describe the way someone spoke but, to be honest, I couldn't think of a better word in this case. She turned and we followed her into Simon's inner sanctum. I couldn't help appreciating Shona's extremely attractive physique, the swaying hips, the long, slender legs, all encased in a tight black mini dress, her red hair hanging in lustrous curls down to her shoulders. I suddenly felt a sharp pain in the ribs.

"Close your mouth," Jan hissed. "You look like a dribbling simpleton."

I did as was asked but couldn't take my eyes off Shona's buttocks. That old song 'Poetry in Motion' could have been written about those buttocks. Men who say things like – I never look at another woman – are liars. All men look at other good-looking women, it's in our DNA, just as women look at fit men. It's natural, why do people get uptight about it. I suppose it's a bit like window shopping, it's nice to look, but you have no intention of buying.

"What a beautiful house," said Jan, giving me another dig in the ribs.

"Eh, oh yeah, very impressive," I said, the polished, oak panelling not even a close second to Shona's sexy wiggle. She stopped suddenly and I nearly knocked her over. "Sorry," I mumbled.

Her laugh was musical and warm. It made the hairs on the back of my neck stand up. She turned and reached forward to open the door she'd stopped in front of. Her left breast brushed my arm and her perfume was as intoxicating as a bottle of scotch. "Simon's in here," she almost whispered, and I nearly drowned in those dark, brown eyes. She opened the door and I, practically, fell into the room.

"Ben, Jan, so glad you could make it. Come in, have an aperitif," said the vicar, his perfect teeth flashing in a charming smile.

"How could we resist," said Jan. If smarming were an Olympic sport, she would have won a gold medal. I almost threw up but then realized she was trying to get her own back for my leching at Shona, who, unfortunately, had left us.

I gave him the best smile I could manage and said, "Good of you to invite us."

"Nonsense," he replied, with a wave of his hand. "As vicar of this parish, I would be very lax in my duties, if I didn't welcome you properly."

"Oh, so it's just duty then?" I said with a nod.

"I think you're trying to twist my words, Ben," he said genially, but I'm sure I saw a hint of irritation in those stormy, baby blues. "Just an expression. I am very happy to have you over for dinner. It's a chance for us to really get to know one another."

This time I did look around, having nothing else to distract me. We were in the library, the walls covered with shelves of books and it only took a cursory glance to assume that quite a few of the tomes on show were, probably, first editions and worth a lot of money. A couple of books, especially, caught my eye, *'The Book of the Law'* and a volume by Aleister Crowley called *'The Book of Lies'* and, although I couldn't remember why these titles disturbed me, I was surprised to find them among the likes of *Dickens, Hardy, Pope* and poetry collections by *Wordsworth, Shelley, Byron* and *Keats*. "A very extensive library," I commented.

"I'm glad you approve, Ben. Books are food for the soul. I'm sure you agree."

"Some," I concurred. "But as Edward Bulwer-Lytton put it in the 1800s – the pen is mightier than the sword. Some literature can incite and, indeed, corrupt."

"Very true, Ben. I look forward to many interesting discussions but, for Jan's sake and, of course, the baby's, shall we eat?"

I nodded, wondering what had happened to the aperitif. As if reading my mind, Simon said, "We'll have our aperitif in the dining room, if that's agreeable?"

I nodded again, beginning to feel like one of those dogs in the backs of cars.

"You have a beautiful house," said Jan.

The vicar smiled and took her arm. "It was built in 1859 for a rather dodgy character named Edward Chanter," he said. "He, apparently, made his fortune from smuggling, both goods and people, the latter sold as slaves throughout the south west. He had this house built to his own, extremely strict specifications – there is supposed to be a secret passageway to the island a small distance from the beach, would you believe?" He laughed. "I've been here five years and I haven't found it, although there are a few within the house itself."

"So, what happened to him?" Jan asked.

"Well, the authorities cottoned on to his illegal activities and closed in on him. If you believe the vague accounts of his final demise, he escaped through this mythical tunnel to 'Smugglers' Rock', that's how it was known."

I remembered my earlier trip to the beach and looking out to the island in question, not realizing its history.

"So, did they nab him on the island?" I asked, unable to hide my curiosity.

"No, no they didn't. They rowed out to the island and searched it thoroughly but found no trace of old 'Edward'. The official conclusion was that he'd realized he was on course for a sizeable prison sentence and thrown himself in the drink.

"I take it they never found his body." Despite my dislike of our host, I was intrigued and would have loved to fire up the laptop later and Google 'Edward Chanter', but as we had no internet connection that would be out of the question.

"No, by all accounts, he disappeared without a trace.

"And what about the village? Who named it 'Chanter's Hide'?" I continued.

"When Chanter built this house, there was no village, that was the whole point. It was somewhere he could conduct his clandestine affairs without detection; or so he thought. The village grew slowly over the next century and records are, again, extremely vague, to say the least. As to when it adopted the name 'Chanter's Hide' – that's not known either." Simon opened the dining room door and we both gasped, I, reluctantly, of course.

Oh, what a gorgeous room," Jan cooed.

I was back in nodding dog mode. "Very nice," I conceded.

"Yes, he may have been a bit of a rogue, but he had an eye for style," said Simon.

The 'bit of a rogue' description disturbed me a little, especially coming from a man of the cloth. He had his hand on Jan's back, just above her buttocks, leading her into the dining room. He turned to me and winked.

Vicars do not wink, that is a fact; like the Queen doesn't get down and shake her booty. There are some things that just don't happen, and a vicar winking is one of them. I have to say, I was about to grab hold of the son of a God when Shona brushed past me; a little too slowly to go without note, her right breast lingering, not unpleasantly, against my left arm, her perfume becoming less alcoholic and more narcotic.

"Come, Ben. Sit." She pulled out a chair and I did as I was told. Jan allowed Simon to usher her to a chair opposite. If I'm honest, I firmly believe she would have followed wherever he led, if you get my meaning. Having said that, I was finding it difficult to remain impartial to Shona's affectionate attention. I was not au fait with the ways of a serving girl but was damned sure she was taking it to the next level. She was good, I'll give her that, and, had I not loved Jan so much, I would have been tempted. But, as I sat there within this pseudo-sexual balloon I, suddenly, realized – it was a game – to see how far we'd go.

"We're not swingers," I said defiantly.

They both burst out laughing. Jan looked shocked.

"What on earth are you talking about, my dear boy?" Simon asked.

I felt about three feet tall, his and Shona's expressions ridiculing me, Jan's filled with disgust.

"Why do you have to spoil everything?" She asked me, tears in her eyes.

"I'm sorry sweetheart, what with the move and everything, and worrying about you two." I gave her a sickly grin and stroked her belly. "I guess I'm losing it a bit."

"You just insulted Simon and Shona, it's not me you should be apologising to."

I muttered a 'sorry' to the pair of them but knew, deep down inside, that there was much more to Simon, Shona, and the rest of Chanter's Hide than met the eye. I know, I've never been the religious sort, but, I maintain, vicars do not wink at male parishioners whilst, practically, cupping said parishioner's wife's buttocks. What's more, vicars do not have housekeepers that put Sophia Loren to shame. It doesn't happen.

Shona smiled and I thanked God she was looking at Jan. Another ridiculous expression came to mind – I could have drowned in those eyes. Suddenly, it didn't seem so ridiculous.

"Shall we eat?" Simon asked. "Shona?"

"Everything's ready to go," she replied, with a smile.

"Good. I hope you're hungry," he said, looking at Jan.

"Absolutely," she answered with a sickly smile.

I nodded and managed a grunt, wondering if I could smell arsenic, that's if arsenic has a smell, of course. I was starting to get on my own nerves with my ridiculous paranoia. I couldn't forget that wink though.

I looked at Jan, shrugged and increased the sickliness of my own smile, my top lip sticking to my teeth. I was doing an incredible job of making a complete idiot of myself.

"How about that aperitif, before Shona brings the starter?" Simon asked, smiling at me, unable to conceal the amusement he was, quite clearly, feeling.

"Jan?"

"Oh, just a tonic water for me," she replied, giving Charlie a pat.

"Ben? I have a fine Amontillado."

Truth be told I could have done with a tumbler of Scotch, the way I was feeling, but accepted the sherry with as much grace as I could summon. It was apparent to me that, even though I was managing beautifully myself, I was having a fair bit of help also, in turning myself into the latest village idiot. I was annoyed that I'd aided the vicar and his fancy piece to make a monkey out of me. If I said anything to Jan about it later, she'd just call me paranoid and tell me to grow up. There were the little 'knowing' looks Simon and Shona gave me from time to time throughout the night when Jan wasn't looking. Looks that said it all.

I tried my best to recover a little of my self-esteem from the sherry onwards, attempting to act like the model dinner guest.

"This is excellent," I said, after tasting the Amontillado and, to be fair, it was rather good. Although things between Jan and I were strained, the vicar was having a great time and by the time Shona brought the starter he was beaming like the proverbial Cheshire cat.

"This is liver pate, made by our very own Sam Templeton; I believe you met him at your welcoming party."

I remembered the farmer, the first 'Hider' we'd set eyes on when entering the village and nodded.

"The brioche, although toasted by Shona, was baked by George Packer, the village baker and the salad is fresh from our very own garden. Enjoy."

We all tucked in, including Shona, and I couldn't fault it. The pate was moist and delicious, the brioche practically melted in the mouth and the salad beautifully dressed and fresh.

"Simple fare," said old George. "But fit for a king, I'm sure you'll agree."

"Very tasty," I concurred.

"I've never tasted pate like it," Jan said enthusiastically. "And the bread was to die for. And the salad – so fresh, and that dressing…." She held her fingers up to pursed lips and, I must admit, I nearly threw up. Jan had never been a creep, she had always called a spade a spade but since meeting this, so called, man of the cloth, her judgement and self-respect seemed to have taken a holiday.

Shona cleared away the plates, all empty, I accede, and Simon poured glasses of a 'cheeky little Merlot' for me, Shona, and himself. Jan stuck with the tonic.

When Shona wheeled in the main course on a large hostess trolley, I started to salivate.

I have, on many occasions, embarked on a vegetarian regime and tried to urge Jan in a similar direction. Unfortunately, she has never seen the eating of meat as anything more than a food chain thing, with man (and woman) hitting the top spot. Her Mum and Dad were never into pets, whereas I saw two Labradors go from puppyhood to old age, watching as their poor, old legs became too weak to support them. It still brings a tear to my eye when I think about the vet coming to the house and leaving with Jake's limp body wrapped in a blanket; I loved that dog. When Sally followed him, a year later, I was at Bristol University and, although sad, I didn't have to witness the life slipping from her eyes, as I had with the old feller. I've always loved animals, especially dogs, the beauty, the simplicity, the dependence they have on us to provide sustenance and warmth. I always feel guilty when I eat meat but try and make myself feel better by telling myself that if I became vegetarian, no animals would be saved. I know - it's a copout.

The huge, silver platter on top of the trolley was a meat eater's dream. There were slices of beef, pork, and lamb. On the second shelf were roast, new and dauphinois potatoes and a selection of fresh vegetables in garlic and cheese sauces. Three silver gravy boats contained, what I believe are now called, jus.

The overall aroma was breath-taking. I was struggling to stop myself from dribbling.

"All of the meat is locally reared, and the vegetables grown here at Chanter House. We pride ourselves in being self-sufficient in the 'Hide'." Simon boasted.

I winced. The term 'Hiders' was bad enough.

"A lot of 'Hiders'," I didn't attempt to disguise my contempt for the expression. "Must, surely, do their big shop at Morrison's in Bridport."

The vicar and his moll looked at me as if I were dog shit that had become embedded in the tread of their brand-new walking boots. "We encourage all members of the village to support the community. To do otherwise is, quite frankly, frowned upon."

I was flabbergasted. "So, if we sneak out and get some Morrison's doughnuts, we'll be flogged. Is that what you're saying?"

"No Ben, you wouldn't be flogged," he said, with a cross between a smile and a sneer. "I just think that once you've tasted everything that the village has to offer, you'll be less inclined to supplement it with salt and vinegar crisps or Doritos, or, indeed, doughnuts."

As Shona served us all with the meat feast, I scrutinised Simon's features and, for the first time, felt more than discomfort. I glanced at Jan, who was nodding her head and hanging on his every word. For a second or two, I wondered if I was being paranoid. Then I remembered what my dad used to say - when in doubt, trust your instinct. My instinct, in this case, told me I wasn't.

We made short work of the main and it was delicious. I would have liked to have found something substandard, but I couldn't. The sweet was a simple summer pudding with all the fruit locally grown, of course. The cream was better than any I'd tasted, again, the work of Farmer Templeton. From what I'd tasted today, the idea of supporting the local community and excluding foreign sources, so to speak, was an attractive one. Had old George not been so forceful in that direction and made it sound more like an order than an option, I would have, probably, been quite keen on the prospect. When someone tells me, I can't do something or tries to make me feel like a leper if I do, I dig my heels in. All men are free to make their own decisions in life, whether they are right or wrong; it is all down to personal choice. The vicar seemed to be trying to take that away, and that just wasn't right, especially for a man of the cloth.

Shona had brought in a chilled Chablis to accompany desert and, once again, it was excellent.

"Do I take it that it's fine to buy wine from outside the village?" I asked, challenging Simon's apparent double standards.

He gave a resigned type of smile, the sort you might use while admonishing a recidivistic child and shook his head. "Joe McGrath, 'The Duck's' landlord not only looks after our beers and lagers, he brews them as well. He also has a fine winery and, although the selection may not be as extensive as you would find in your local supermarket, the quality is far better. The climate we enjoy, here in the south west, is exceedingly kind to the vines. In fact, the only beverage sold in our local not produced by Joe is the cider, and Sam takes care of that. So, you see, we are totally self-sufficient."

"What about electricity? I'm sure Joe or Sam can't produce that," I said, unable to curb a smug grin.

The vicar smiled back. "Well, I suppose, in a way, Sam does. You see, the south side of both of his barns are made up of solar panels. I'm not sure of the technical details, but those and power generated by methane keep the village running nicely. Throughout the summer months much more electricity is produced than we need, the residue is stored and supplements the short fall throughout the winter." His smile widened; mine disappeared. The bastard had an answer for everything.

I knew when I was beaten. I spent the rest of the evening, keeping it zipped, nodding, and utilising my best false smile when required. Both Jan and I declined cheese and biscuits and went straight to the coffee, a chicory-based concoction (grown in the vicar's garden) that hit the spot. I was getting really pissed off with liking everything produced 'locally'. I longed to be served something that was a little bit iffy. At least the brandy wasn't another of Joe's creations, several bottles had been left in the cellar by the previous owner, along with the sherry I'd sampled earlier. So, although not locally produced, it hadn't been brought in from outside by any existing 'Hiders'. So, I guess that made it all right.

By the time we came to leave, it was nearly midnight. The sky was awash with stars, the moon, a silver beacon. On the coast, without city pollution the firmament is a beautiful sight, a blanket of stunning clarity. I breathed in the sea air, relieved to be saying goodnight to the vicar and his moll.

"When we're sorted, you'll have to come to us," Jan said.

I nodded. "Indeed," I said, not quite as eagerly as my wife.

"Plenty of time," said Simon. "I know how stressful it is to lay down new roots and make a house your own. Take your time and make sure the little one doesn't become distressed." He waved his hand in the direction of Jan's bump and then looked at me. "You make sure you look after them both, Ben."

Once again, I felt the statement to be more of an order than a piece of friendly banter.

"Don't worry, I will," I said sharply.

He grinned, that irritating – I love winding you up – type grin. "I know you will, young man."

My fists clenched and I really wanted to punch the patronizing bastard in the face. He knew he was pushing my buttons; I knew he was, but I couldn't help rising to the bait. I was as angry with myself as I was with him.

"Well, goodnight and thanks for a wonderful meal." I grabbed Jan's arm and nearly dragged her down the drive.

She pulled free, glaring at me. "Oh, Simon, you couldn't recommend a good plumber, could you? Our water flow isn't as good as it should be."

The vicar laughed. "I'm afraid the plumbing is ancient and the whole village could do with an upgrade, but it isn't financially viable. Unfortunately, we can't barter with the water companies, they need hard cash. I'm afraid it would cost a small fortune to bring our waterworks up to date. I guess we're all used to it."

Jan smiled, "I suppose we will have to be, as well then. It's been a lovely evening; we must return the compliment." I gave a half-hearted smile and guided Jan down the driveway. When we reached the road, she pulled her arm away and glared at me.

"What has got into you lately?" She snarled. "You're acting like a madman. God knows what Simon and Shona thought. At times, you were downright rude."

"There's something not right," I said, frowning. "Vicars don't wink, for a start."

"What are you talking about?" She suddenly looked concerned. "I'm starting to worry about you."

"You didn't see him," I said. "All night he was taking the piss out of me and schmoozing you. And, another thing, how many vicars have you seen with a 'housekeeper' like her?" I emphasized the word housekeeper, indicating it was a euphemism.

"You really are becoming fixated and paranoid; I've never known you like this."

"You just can't see past his George Clooney looks and false charm," I moaned.

Jan sighed. "Not this rubbish again, please."

I sighed. "You'll see."

"What, Ben. What will I see?" She stopped, her hands on her hips, a combination of anger and worry flashing in her beautiful, brown eyes.

I shook my head. "I don't know yet. Come on let's go home, it's been a long night."

SIX

We walked back in silence. I was obviously in the doghouse. I couldn't understand why she didn't see anything wrong with our recently acquired man of the cloth. She seemed besotted. By the time we reached our gate, my mind was racing, and I knew I wouldn't sleep. I walked up and unlocked the front door.

"I'm going for a walk," I told Jan. "I need to clear my head."

"I'll second that," she said, going in and slamming the door.

I mumbled a few expletives and wandered back down the street. I looked up and watched a wisp of cloud creep gingerly across the face of the moon, like a cat sneaking past a sleeping dog. A faint breeze eased the humidity as I turned toward the sea. I loved this part of the world and was disappointed that I didn't feel at home here. I wondered if my feelings for Simon would change in time and I would see him the way Jan did. At that precise moment in time, it seemed highly unlikely. I couldn't get that wink out of my head. It was the kind that said – I've got your wife wrapped around my little finger and there's nothing you can do about it. And he was right; the more I tried to persuade her, he was a wrong 'un, the more she dug in her heels and defended him. The more I became a suitable case for treatment. He had some sort of agenda, I was sure of it, and it wasn't Godly, of that, I was almost certain.

The reflection of the moon in the quiet ripples meandering slowly to the shore was a sight to warm anyone's cockles. After the poor 480p picture of Knightsbridge at midnight, the 1080p high definition of Dorset always blew me away. It was like going from a crabby old VHS recorder to a Blu-ray player. It was because of this I saw the light bobbing along on 'Smugglers' Rock'. Someone was, obviously, carrying some sort of torch or lantern. This was becoming more and more sinister by the hour. I was starting to feel trapped in some old Hammer film. Who would be wandering about on an island in the middle of the night, but, more importantly, why? Even though the temperature hadn't dropped even a fraction of a degree, I shivered. What had we moved into here? If I said anything to Jan, she'd reiterate her concerns about my paranoia and be even more worried that I was hallucinating. I squinted trying to make out more than the light, but, even with HD, the distance foiled my less than 20/20 vision. I turned my head, to get a better view and nearly jumped out of my skin. It was the sad boy's father, the moon showing the lines in his face, a visage that had been shaved to within an inch of its life. His eyes were sharp and blue, appraising me.

"You must be old Ted's nephew," he said in a broad west-country accent, reminding me of The Wurzels.

"I am," I said, holding out my hand. He ignored it.

"Ted was a good man," he said. "We were good friends, he and I."

He turned and walked back to the village, leaving me standing there, hand outstretched, still waiting to be shaken. I turned back to the island. The light was gone.

I sat on the beach for another hour or so, gazing out at 'Smugglers' Rock', waiting for the light to reappear. It didn't. I thought about Uncle Ted's old friend, and his son. Both had appeared at their cottage window as we were on our way to the pub, but neither had joined our welcoming committee. After our brief encounter, he didn't seem like a typical 'Hider'. From what I remembered of Uncle Ted, I couldn't see him as part of this pseudo-Utopian, self-sufficient, cliquish community either. If memory served me well, he was a miserable sod who didn't have a good word for anybody. I, certainly, couldn't see him getting on with smarmy Simon. I decided that I needed to call on Ted's old buddy and have a chat. Hopefully, I could meet the boy as well. We'd only been here a couple of days but, already, I was feeling pressured to conform. To become a smiley, gushing member of this worrying, close-knit brotherhood. I suppose, I was looking for an ally, someone to prove to me, I wasn't just imagining things.

I stood up and started back to the cottage. Jan would be fast asleep by now and I didn't want to disturb her. I'd stay downstairs and stick my headphones on. Maybe a bit of Tom Waits' unique growl would settle me. I'd keep it low; I had a pair of Grado cans but, although the sound quality was excellent, the noise containment wasn't brilliant. I tended to rack up the volume and irritate Jan, at times. So tonight, or should I say, this morning, Tom's dulcet tones would have to be quieter than normal.

I crept up the garden path and opened the door as quietly as possible. I opened the laptop and clicked on Spotify, I heard Jan get out of bed and pad across the landing to the loo. I waited for her to flush and get back into bed before I carried on. It wasn't until the message came up telling me there was no internet access that I remembered about the lack of broadband. I closed the laptop, sat back, and closed my eyes. Suddenly they had become heavy. Within seconds I was asleep, and my dreams were plagued with vicars. First there was old George Clooney, dog collar shining like a slipped halo. Chuck Berry was next, complete with guitar and Berry strut, followed by Bill Clinton and Boris Johnson doing a tango. All three wore dog collars, even though old Boris was buck naked. Vincent Price entered stage left with Peter Lorre under his arm. The procession carried on, whilst Margaret Thatcher stood on a pedestal singing Tom Wait's songs. I was just enjoying a bit of pole dancing by a dog collared Cher when Jan shook me.

"It's eight o'clock," she said.

I was still in the doghouse, by the sound of it.

"Right," I said. "I'm going to grab a shower."

There was no response. While I was under the dribble, I wondered if I needed to start thinking about redecorating this kennel. I had the feeling I was going to be spending a lot of time in it.

As I was drying myself off, the unmistakable smell of sizzling bacon wafted up the stairs. My stomach growled and my mouth watered; I was suddenly, famished. I began to wonder if my stay in the canine cottage included meals up at the big house. I pulled on a pair of khaki shorts and a plain white T shirt and headed down to investigate.

As I entered the kitchen, Jan was placing a plate of bacon, sausage, eggs, tomatoes, and mushrooms on the table.

"Is that for me?" I almost pleaded.

"Not that you deserve it, "she replied sternly.

"Look, this is ridiculous," I said. "I don't want us to fall out. We've just moved into a new house, for Christ's sake."

She looked me in the eye. "I don't want any of this either," she said. "You've really got to get these stupid ideas out of your head, you know."

I was about to retaliate but thought about the greater good. I smiled and nodded. "Yeah, you're right. Maybe it's all the hassle of the move. They do say that moving to a new house is one of the most stressful things you can go through."

That brought a slight smile. "Eat your breakfast before it gets cold. I went to Ena's while you were still kipping and bought it all fresh. All local produce, off course."

With the 'local produce' remark, I nearly went off on one, but, instead, jammed another forkful of sausage and egg in my mouth, chewed slowly and said. "Is she nice, Ena?"

"All of the 'Hiders' call the shop Ena's," she said with a grin. "She's a lovely woman, ever so helpful. She keeps a record of everything everyone brings in, so she knows what they're due in return. It works really well, apparently. You won't forget you've got to pop in for an hour or so and help her out, will you?"

"I'll do it tomorrow, my sweet."

"Make sure you do. Most folks around here grow their own veg. As Simon said, the farmers supply the meat. It's a real community. Once you've got that jungle sorted out, we'll have to start growing lettuce and tomatoes and cucumber, maybe some onions. You'll like Ena."

Along with the piece of bacon, I was munching on, I also bit my tongue. It was becoming difficult. "I'm sure I will," I said. Inside I was seething; Jan was using the dreaded term as well now. I began to wonder if it was some sort of brainwashing that I was, somehow, immune to. I vowed to show her the error of her ways. I was still convinced that all was not peace and love in Chanter's Hide. Until I had concrete proof, however, I would pretend to be a reluctant convert. We finished our breakfast in silence and I have to admit, it was bloody delicious. It was as if someone had taken an excellent hotel breakfast and magnified the flavours tenfold. I was finding it extremely difficult to fault the self-sufficiency of the village.

I did the washing up as Jan unpacked more boxes upstairs. I decided to attack the back garden again once I'd finished. Looking at it through the kitchen window, in its present state, would soon piss Jan off. I tried to embrace the jungle look but, even I, had to wince. It was a mess. I put the last of the crockery in the cupboard, put my watch back on, took a deep breath and opened the back door. Time to become Tarzan.

I wandered out to the old shed, took up my trusty scythe and gave it another going over with the pumice stone. Considering its age, I managed to get a keen edge on it. I attacked the garden with gusto (wasn't he one of the Marx Brothers?) and as I reduced the level of the vegetation even further, I started to get a taste for the old gardening lark. I found myself imagining flower beds and Jan's vegetable patches and even a water feature, maybe. The sun was high in a cloudless sky and the sweat poured out of me at an alarming rate. I made frequent visits to the kitchen for water to replace the gallons leaking from my skin. It was a good feeling to be physically productive and I forgot all about my nemesis, the vicar. As I worked away, I lost all track of time and was shocked when Jan called me in for lunch. I looked at my watch; it was twelve thirty.

I walked in through the back door and Jan was holding a towel and pointing towards the sink. Her nose was turned up in disgust.

"Wash some of the muck and sweat off, before you sit down," she said.

"Are you sure you don't want me to take a shower?" I asked flippantly.

"No. You'll be going back out there after lunch, so it would be pointless and a waste of water."

I turned on the cold tap and, suddenly, thought – water. Where does the village get its water from? I dried my hands and face and sat at the kitchen table. Jan had made ham salad sandwiches, with mustard. Two large sausage rolls sat on one plate in the centre of the table, a couple of her homemade scones on another, complete with pots of whipped cream and jam.

"Everything, apart from the scones are from Ena's," she said proudly.

I ignored the remark. "Where does Chanter's Hide get its water from?" I asked her. "They can't grow that."

"Don't be stupid," she snapped. "There's a reservoir in the hills behind the village. Apparently, the pipe work has been here for years. Sam and Joe do their best to keep it running. There's a pumping station on Sam's farm. The 'Hiders' don't advocate wasting water though."

I felt deflated. "Of course, they don't," I said.

Jan sighed. "You're not going to start again, are you?"

I bit my tongue again and shook my head. "No, darling, 'course I'm not. I just wondered, that's all."

"Good, now eat your lunch and then get back to work. I want to be able to sit out in that garden and enjoy some of the summer," she said, with a nod.

"Hold on," I protested. "I'm not Percy Thrower, remember. There's a lot work involved. I doubt that........"

She burst out laughing. "I'm joking, you idiot. Although I don't know who Percy Thrower is or was, I'm guessing he was a much better gardener than you."

I pushed out my bottom lip and tried to look hurt. "I'm doing my best, Ma'am."

She laughed harder and I joined her. I vowed there and then that whatever old George Clooney was up to, it wasn't going to come between Jan and me. I would tow the village line until I had some concrete evidence of shady goings on.

By the time I'd finished one of Jan's wonderful scones, smothered in local cream and strawberry jam, I was stuffed.

"That jam is to die for," Jan said, closing her eyes.

It pained me to admit it, but it was extremely tasty. Even the cream was creamier. All of Chanter's Hide's produce screamed decadence. The villagers should all be obese, but from what I'd seen on our first night, there wasn't an ounce of fat on most of them. Apart from the landlady's substantial bosom and George Plummer's rosy, bulbous proboscis, I couldn't recall any beer bellies or anyone bordering on the plump. Even George's brother Joe, the landlord, although massive, was solid muscle.

I pushed my chair back and patted my belly. "That'll keep me going for a while," I said. "A lovely lunch, sweetheart. The scones were the best part, of course."

"Go on," Jan replied, with a huge grin. "Get that garden sorted out. I want it fit for a queen."

I touched my forelock. "Yes Ma'am."

I returned to my toil, feeling replete and in a reasonable place mentally. I could see how the charm of the vicar and his moll and the friendliness of the villagers, combined with the fine food they managed to produce could influence the best. Maybe I was a naturally suspicious sort. As Jan had already pointed out my character judgement was a little flawed. Then that wink came back to haunt me, and I shook my head – vicars do not wink at women's husbands whilst their hand is practically squeezing the wife's arse.

I let my frustration out on the weeds, swinging that scythe like a demented Alan Titchmarsh. After about half an hour I took off my sodden T shirt and continued topless, the sun's rays simultaneously drying and producing sweat. Jan called to me a little later, leaving a jug of ice cube laden orange squash outside the back door with a glass.

"There you go He-man."

I spread out my arms, still gripping the scythe, showing off my sweaty, anaemic-looking torso and gave her my best Tarzan war cry. She laughed and went back inside.

I carried on for another ten minutes or so, until I was parched. I poured myself a glass of squash and it didn't touch the sides. I refilled the glass and sat on the path my back, against the wall by the door. Luckily, the sun had travelled, and this part of the garden was now shaded. The bricks, although not cool, weren't the hot coals they'd probably been an hour ago. As I sat sipping my second glass of orange, I remembered the metal box I'd found in the shed and decided, after I'd had a little rest, I'd try and get the bugger open. It'd probably be full of old nuts and bolts or something, but, if so, why would it be locked? In situations like that the old curiosity gets the better of a person. I drained my glass, stretched my aching muscles, stood, and wandered back down to the shed. The box was on the shelf where I'd left it - why wouldn't it be? I rummaged through the pile of tools and found a flat blade screwdriver that had seen better days but might suffice. I attacked the lock. The screwdriver slipped and grazed my hand and I swore. I put the box on the floor, sideways, put my foot on it and re-applied the screwdriver. I eased it into the slit between the lid and the base and leant on it. There was a click and the lid sprang open. I picked it up and looked in. There, on a bed of velvet, was a strange looking pendant. It appeared to be, what I believed was the Star of David, with one of those Egyptian symbols, like a cross with a loop at the top, fixed into the space in the centre. I took it out; it was heavy and, obviously, solid gold. I wondered what miserable, Uncle Ted was doing with some weird talisman.

I sat on the floor of the shed, staring at the thing, wondering what it meant and why it was there. I thought about asking Ted's old pal if he knew anything. In my former life we'd published a couple of novels by a guy who thought he was the next Dennis Wheatley. Unfortunately, for us as well as him, they didn't sell anywhere near as well as Dennis' had. As novels went, they weren't half bad and I think, if the company had shelled out for a bit of promotion, they could have done reasonably well. As it was, they bombed and, I'm sorry to admit, I couldn't even remember the author's name. The stories, I seemed to recall, relied heavily on the use of pentagrams, crosses, stars, and other paraphernalia, in their quest to defeat the horned one. I laughed out loud; what the hell was the matter with me. We had moved into a village where everyone was so efficient and self-sufficient, it made me sick, that was true enough. But, on second thoughts, was it? Or was it just that the damned vicar wouldn't stop ramming it down my throat. Looked at logically, the villagers had to be praised for their ingenuity and resourcefulness. Only a numbskull would decry their achievements and, as far as the produce was concerned, the quality was beyond reproach. Since we'd arrived in Chanter's Hide, I had been so focused on Simon bloody Drake that I had failed to look at the bigger picture and now, I was throwing Black Magic into the pot. I decided, there and then, to stop allowing my feelings for old George to taint everything else the village had to offer. Dodgy vicars, let's face it, are not unusual. If I had as little to do with him as possible and tried to get on with my life, maybe, in time, even the term 'Hiders' wouldn't irritate me as much – maybe. I still wanted to talk to Uncle Ted's mate and meet his son, though. The boy's sad face still haunted me, and I had to find out why he seemed so melancholy. I still couldn't get that pleading expression out of my mind. I'm sure I wasn't mistaken; he was asking for help.

I put the pendant back in the box and sighed. I heaved my aching limbs to a standing position and looked at my watch. It was 5.10 p.m. I put the scythe and pumice stone back in the shed, closed the door and walked up the path. It was time for a shower, a long one. Time to let the feeble spray wash away the day's toil and warm the sore muscles. It was official, I was a soft-handed office boy. I glanced at my scythe hand and was quite proud to see a blister at the base of my index finger. War wound.

Jan was busy at the oven when I entered the kitchen, the aroma escaping, delightful.

"That smells gorgeous," I said enthusiastically.

She closed the oven door, turned, and grinned. "Steak and kidney pie," she said proudly. "And it's looking good if I do say so myself. It'll be ready in half an hour; you better get a wriggle on."

I winked at her. "On my way, darling wife."

We enjoyed a wonderful meal. Not taking anything away from Jan's cooking, but doesn't it always taste better after a hard day's graft. It's as if you've earned it. I ate so much pie, with mash, peas, and lashings of gravy that I had no room for any pudding, which was a shame because Jan's strawberry tart looked beautiful. Instead, we drank the last of the coffee that we'd brought with us. I was still a little reluctant to admit, that it paled into insignificance compared to the stuff we'd tasted at the vicar's.

"Have you decided what you're going to do with the garden?" She asked me.

"I'm open to suggestions. I was thinking about a small vegetable patch on one side of the path."

Jan looked incredulous. "Do you think you can manage that? Are you actually turning into Perry Thrower?"

"Percy," I corrected her. "Perry was a singer, I think. Perry Comb-over, my Dad used to call him. I can't remember what his real name was."

"Perry Como," Jan said with a wistful smile. "My gran loved him. He had quite a nice voice, as I recall. One of the old crooners, like Bing Crosby and Nat thingamajig."

"King Cole," I said.

"That's the feller."

I drained my cup, patted my belly, and sighed. "After that sumptuous meal, you go and put your feet up and I'll do the washing up. Afterwards we can get that 'Orange is the New Black' box set out and watch an episode or two if you like."

"Sounds like a plan," Jan said with a grin. "I'm glad you've stopped all the silly stuff about Simon and that."

Even though I'd sworn to change my attitude and give the place a chance, his name was like a knife in my guts. I managed to hide my feelings, put on a brave face and a suitable smile. I added a wink, for good measure.

"Don't nod off, you know what you're like," I said.

She gave me a salute. "No sir."

I took the dishes into the kitchen and filled the sink with hot water. As I worked, my thoughts returned to the strange pendant in the shed. Ordinarily, something like that wouldn't have bothered me. It was just, knowing what I knew about Uncle Ted, plus what my dad used to say about him, it was totally out of character. In fact, the whole Chanter's Hide ethos didn't fit. If I were having trouble with the commune-type philosophy, he certainly would have had. He was a dedicated loner. Still, having said that, he'd obviously become matey with one of the residents. It suddenly occurred to me that the vicar had never mentioned Ted once, not when he welcomed us to the village, nor at the pub, nor, indeed, during the hours we spent at his place having dinner. That was odd, in itself. I needed to speak to his old buddy. Tomorrow, I decided – definitely.

When I went back into the lounge Jan was fast asleep in the armchair, the DVD box set on her lap. I shook her gently and told her to go to bed. She yawned, nodded, and headed for the stairs. I told her I'd be up soon. I picked up the laptop and my headphones. A bit of Ben Howard might do the trick. Once again, I'd forgotten about the lack of internet. I grabbed my iPod and chose the playlist I'd named 'Smooth'. I shoved the earphones into my lugs and sat back. I would have to find out about the Wi-Fi, even if it meant asking Drake.

SEVEN

I awoke just after 1.00 a.m. Ben and his mates had packed up their guitars and vacated the iPod a while ago. I was just switching it off when I remembered Edward Chanter. I nearly picked the laptop back up and typed the name in the search bar. You don't realise how much you use the internet until you don't have it. I suddenly felt totally cut off. No mobile signal, no internet, how was a man meant to survive? I had to admit, when I'd mentioned broadband to the solicitor dealing with Uncle Ted's affairs, he'd been pretty non-committal, much like the Wi-Fi now. Normally a list of networks close by would appear, even if they were password protected. My laptop was picking up nothing. Surely someone in the village had internet access, even if it wasn't the fastest. I made a mental note to ask one of the villagers – preferably not the vicar – who their provider was. This, in turn, turned my thoughts to electricity and water. The village provided both, apparently, but, so far, there had been no mention of charges. Then I began to think about money. I had about forty quid in my wallet and I know Jan had a similar amount in her purse, when we'd arrived. Since then, she'd bought quite a few items from the local shop. Was there a cash machine in Chanter's Hide or did we have to drive into Bridport? There was no two ways about it, this place was bizarre. I crept upstairs, undressed in the dark and slipped under the duvet as gently as possible. Jan stirred and mumbled something in her sleep, then was dead to the world again. I lay there for ages, my arm behind my head. Too many things were racing around my brain. I still couldn't understand why Jan had just accepted all the weird shit that was going on around us without any qualms. Normally, she was a natural sceptic, but she'd swallowed this 'Good Life' stuff hook, line, and sinker. Nowhere could be so perfect and so self-sufficient. I resolved to get to the bottom of whatever it was that was going on here. If it turned out that Chanter's Hide was the perfect village and was all above board, I'd be happier than her. My gut was far from convinced.

I closed my eyes, emptied my mind, focusing on an imaginary dot in the centre of my mental vision, slowing my breathing. It was a trick I'd learnt when I was gainfully employed and feeling the stress of too much work and too little sleep. A friend who practised yoga had put me onto it. It took some time to master, I confess. Emptying your mind isn't easy, especially when there are so many worries clamouring for your attention. But I persevered and slowly, night after night, another door was closed until all that was left was that small, imaginary dot.

I closed the last door, the cottage with the overgrown garden and the boy at the window and fell into a troubled sleep.

The following morning, the weather began to break. The sky was grey with cloud, rain forecast for the afternoon. After a breakfast of cereal and toast, I decided to have a couple of hours on the garden before calling on Ted's old friend. Jan was going to make the final touches to the move. Already, more or less everything was in its place; she had the uncanny knack of accomplishing a huge amount of work, without appearing to put in any effort. If it were me, I'd be dashing everywhere, puffing, and blowing, covered in sweat. I guess it's one of the differences between the sexes – women get on with things with the minimum of fuss, men like everyone to know how hard they're working. Obviously, that doesn't apply to every female and male, but I think it has resonance with a lot of us.

I was so involved in trying to complete my hacking, that I didn't look at the time until it was 11.30 a.m. I went into the house, had a super quick shower and was back in the kitchen by 11.45. Jan was cutting lining paper for the cupboards, a thing I'd never really got a handle on.

"Why do you do that?" I asked her.

She looked at me with a puzzled expression. "Because my mum always used to do it, I suppose."

"What's the point?"

"Well it's.......cleaner, more.......hygienic," she blustered.

"Okay," I said with a grin. "I just wondered."

"Anyway, where are you going?"

"I told you I met that bloke; said he was a mate of Uncle Ted's. I thought I might pop and see him. He probably knew the old bugger better than anyone."

She smiled and nodded. "That would be a nice gesture. Kind of neighbourly. I thought you were going to Ena's today, though."

"I was, wasn't I? I'll go there first." I gave her a kiss. "See you later, gorgeous."

"Lunch about 2.00, okay?" She called as I was going through the front door. I waved a hand in agreement and left.

As I walked down to High Street, I felt the first spots of the promised rain. It must be said, weather forecasts are more reliable these days than they used to be. I reached 'Ena's' and opened the door. The place was like a throwback to the fifties, there was even a pair of old-fashioned scales on the counter with various weights piled up at its side. The smell in the shop was a mixture of fresh vegetables, fruit, and a yeasty kind of odour. It wasn't unpleasant. A small woman came into the shop from out of the back and I vaguely recognised her from our welcoming party. Her hair was tied back and flecked with grey, her features soft and genial.

"Hello Ben, are you here to do your wife's penance?" She smiled and it lit up her face.

"That's about the size of it – Ena?"

"The one and only. Would you like a coffee first?"

"That would be very nice, thanks Ena."

She went into the back again and I heard a kettle heating up. If first impressions were anything to go by, I liked our local shopkeeper. She was nice and seemed to possess a sense of humour. I looked around the shop, as I waited for the coffee. There were boxes propped up against the counter with potatoes, carrots, onions, parsnips, leeks, swede – every vegetable I could think of, but then I'm not an authority. On the counter were punnets of strawberries, blackberries, raspberries, blackcurrants, redcurrants. There were also apples, oranges, and grapefruit. The shelves behind the counter held bags of flour, eggs, jars of jam, marmalade and even honey. There were bottles of coffee, the chicory mixture, I assumed I'd sampled at Drake's.

"Here we go." Ena came back with two steaming mugs. "I'm afraid we don't have any sugar in the village but if you want it sweetened, I can add some honey."

"No, I'm good thanks Ena, gave up sugar about five years ago. Who keeps bees then?"

"I've got a small apiary in the garden out back," she said. "I love my bees."

"Don't you ever get stung?"

"Bees will only sting if they are threatened. Don't forget – if they sting, they die. No, if you look after them, they look after you. There is nothing like fresh honey, it knocks all of your processed stuff into a cocked hat."

"I'm surprised you've tried the processed stuff; the vicar has already told us how self-sufficient you are." I took a sip of my coffee; it was just as good as Drake's.

"I haven't always lived here," she said, looking down.

"Oh, where were you before?"

"We're encouraged not to speak of the past," she said, not looking up.

"By whom?" I knew the answer but wanted to hear her say it.

"It's just a village rule, that's all. We live in the present and look to the future. It doesn't do to dwell on the past."

"We all have memories."

She looked up suddenly and smiled. It was a false, tired, unhappy smile. "I've just realised, Joe came in and moved everything around for me. There's really nothing for you to do. Tell your wife, the cream, jam, and eggs are on the house. It's been nice to meet you, Ben, but I really must get on."

"I can help, surely."

"No, really, I'm fine. All I have to do is prepare a few pork chops and make some mince for the sausages. There's absolutely nothing for you to do. Thanks all the same." She left me standing in the shop and went into the back again. I toyed with the idea of following her and pressing her a little more on Chanter's Hide's peculiar rules and regulations but decided against it. When I had questioned her about her life prior to moving to the village, she'd seemed both sad and frightened. It was as if she yearned to return to those days. I may have misread the situation completely, of course, but I didn't think so.

As I now had time to kill before lunch, I decided to try Ted's old friend. I hurried to the cottage where I'd seen him and the boy. The curtains were pulled to in all three front windows. It was now five minutes shy of noon. I shrugged and walked up the path, pushing my way through the overgrown privet and weeds. The knocker on the door was rusted and immoveable. I rapped three times on the wood and waited. I stood there for a couple of minutes before trying again, banging louder this time. After another few minutes I was still standing looking at the peeling green paint. By this time, the rain was becoming a little more persistent. I walked back up the path and was about to turn for home when a voice behind stopped me.

"Hey Ben, fancy a pint?"

It was Nick, with the lop-sided grin. He was about to go into the pub. I had a couple of hours before lunch would be ready, so I nodded. I could pump him for more info on the village and ask him about the chap who appeared to have been Ted's buddy.

I joined him at the door, and we went in. Joe, the Geoff Capes look-a-like, was polishing the bar; we were his first customers of the day, by the look of it.

"How do gents," he said with a wide grin. He was already pulling a pint of best.

"I know Nick's poison," he added. "If I'm not mistaken, you got yourself outside of a few pints of best, the other night Ben. D'you fancy a re-match?"

"Two at the most, today," I said. "Jan's getting lunch ready for 2.00."

Joe ground his thumb on the bar and the pair of them had a good old chuckle.

I held up my hands. "That's me, chaps. Well and truly under the thumb." I joined in the laughter, hoping it sounded sincere.

Nick was, apparently, still well in credit with Joe, so no payment was made. It was a shame as I wanted to see how this self-sufficiency system worked. I'd expected Nick to pull a couple of rabbits out of his pocket and do a bit of bartering. This place was about as near to Utopia as anywhere could be.

"Cheers Nick," I said, taking a swig. "Do you want to take the weight off? I've been bent double, scything the back garden all morning."

"Er....sure."

I went to a table at the back of the pub and plonked myself down. I wanted to be as far away from flapping ears as possible. Nick sat opposite, took a long swig, and let out a satisfied sigh.

"Yeah," I agreed. "Got to be the best bitter I've ever tasted, and only a rabbit a pint. I can't believe it."

Nick laughed. "You must be joking; a rabbit would get you three. How much is beer in your world?"

"Over a fiver a pint," I said, taking another mouthful.

"Bloody hell," he said, with a shake of his head. "I'm assuming that's expensive?"

I looked at him. "You don't know what a fiver is?"

"Well, not really. In Chanter's Hide, when someone does something for someone else or supplies something but doesn't need anything in return, they get paid with tokens."

"Where do they come from? I mean, Chanter's Hide doesn't have its own mint, does it?"

He looked at me as if I were talking Russian. "Mint?"

"You know, where money is produced."

"I don't know what you're talking about."

It was my turn to be confused. "Surely you've been outside Chanter's Hide? You must have heard of 'The Bank of England'."

He shook his head again. "No, why would I want to?" He asked me, and then added. "Especially, if you've got to pay over a fiver for a pint."

This was getting weirder and weirder. It was obvious that Nick had no clue what I was talking about. I found it unbelievable that he hadn't heard of 'The Bank of England'; everybody knows about 'The Bank of England'.

"Who produces your tokens then?"

"What do you mean, who produces them?"

I was fighting a losing battle. I decided to change the subject.

"Still, this is a bit of a weird place, eh?" I said, knowing I'd be wasting my time. Nick was one of the original Stepford husbands, he'd already made that quite clear.

"How do you mean?"

"Well, everything's a bit too good to be true, don't you think? It's like the Good Life on speed."

If he'd looked confused before, he appeared positively bewildered now. It was as if I'd lapsed back into Russian.

"There's a well-known saying – people don't appreciate what they've got until they lose it," he said stiffly. He was shutting down. I was attacking his precious village. I decided to try him on Uncle Ted's old mate before I alienated him completely.

"Do you know the old chap who lives in the cottage down the street? The one, with the overgrown garden. I think he's got a son."

"Efram Stein. He's not really one of us," he replied flatly.

"What do you mean, not one of us?"

"He's not a 'Hider'," he answered, with a nod and a disgusted expression.

Pardon my French, but the phrase that came to mind was – thank fuck.

We finished our pints and Nick bought another. I think that was the first time I'd never stood my round. Before moving to Chanter's Hide, I'd never been able to leave a pub, knowing I owed someone a drink. It'd caused me no end of problems in the past, as Jan would testify. The thing that annoyed me was that I had money on the hip.

"Sorry, I don't have any tokens, Nick?"

"Not a problem, Ben." He put the pints on the table and smiled. He took out four yellow, plastic tokens and handed them to me. They resembled the counters from a game of 'Connect 4'. "There you go, they'll get you started."

I looked at them with a mixture of confusion and amusement. "Thank you."

I took a sip and sat down. This place was becoming stranger and stranger. There was no chance of me staying after this one. Nick was a 'Hider' through and through, accepting everything about the place without question. I asked him about the broadband and all I got was a blank expression and a shrug.

"What's broadband?" He asked me.

I suddenly wondered if he was winding me up and scrutinised his features, but no, he was deadly serious. "Surely you've got a computer."

"What would I need one of those things for?"

At least he'd heard of them. "How do you find things out?"

He looked puzzled. "Like what?"

This was surreal. In the age of the technological eruption, it seemed we had managed to find the only place in the British Isles that had slipped under the net. It was obvious Nick had led the most sheltered of sheltered lives. I decided there was no point in probing him any further, I might as well talk to the wall.

After exhausting the weather and finding out he had little interest in anything else, we lapsed into silence. I was just draining my glass when the door opened and in walked my favourite person. He sauntered over to our table, looking more like a film star than ever. Not a hair was out of place, he wore a jacket of dark, blue velvet, a matching silk shirt, containing his pristine, whiter than white dog collar and a pair of pale blue slacks.

"Good afternoon gentleman, can I get you a refill?"

"I think I could manage one more, Simon," replied Nick, grinning like the proverbial Cheshire cat.

"Not for me, thanks," I said. I looked at my watch, not really noticing the time. The gesture was all I needed. "Jan will have lunch ready."

The vicar nodded. "Very commendable, Ben." He looked at Nick. "You ought to take a leaf out of his book, young man," he said with a feeble pretence at sternness. It was enough to fool Nick.

"Er…Hannah…erm…. told me," he started to bluster, rising to his feet.

"I'm joking, Nick," Simon said softly, a sickly grin plastered across his chops. "Sit back down, I'll bring it over."

This particular 'Hider' did as his master bade and plonked himself back on the stool, letting out a sigh of relief.

I shook my head. "You're scared of him," I muttered incredulously. "Scared of your own vicar."

He was just about to start blustering again when I felt the vicar's breath on the back of my neck. That was too close for comfort. I stood up and stepped back.

"It's the wrath of the Lord, he's afraid of," Simon said, the grin still in place. "And the wrath of Hannah. Eh, Nick?"

The pathetic man joined in the vicar's false laughter and I was nearly, physically, sick.

"I'll see you later," I said to no-one in particular, walking to the door. As I passed Joe, I was confused by the look on his face. It was like a cross between hope and fear. I shrugged and left. I stopped outside Efram's place. The curtains were still drawn. I thought about trying the door again but turned for home instead. The one crumb of comfort I had gained today was that, Uncle Ted's old buddy wasn't a 'Hider'. If that was the case, Ted, probably hadn't been either. I headed back for lunch, a slight spring in my step. I might have an ally, after all.

EIGHT

As we ate lunch, I told Jan I'd been to Ena's and she'd told me there was nothing to do and the stuff she'd given Jan was on the house. I didn't tell her about our conversation with regards to the past, I couldn't see the point. I said that I had tried but not managed to meet Ted's mate but discovered his name was Efram Stein, over a couple of pints with Nick. She was pleased I was socialising with the villagers, especially Nick. I think she had an idea of the four of us getting together, as she and Hannah were both mums to be. It was understandable. I didn't pop her bubble by mentioning how downright irritating I found Hannah's old man. If we went out for a drink together and Jan and Hannah got firmly ensconced in baby talk, I think I'd rather join in than try and strike up a conversation with Nick. As I've already pointed out, his mental capacity was limited, to say the least; and as I didn't wish to discuss the virtues of the marvellous 'Hiders', a parlance of any description would be difficult. I also failed to touch on the vicar's appearance, I thought it better that way.

"You could have stayed a bit longer, you know," Jan said. "I wouldn't have minded."

"I was tempted," I lied. "But I thought I'd show my wife a good husband, so I had to drag myself away."

"I take it you couldn't find one."

"Very droll."

She finished her sandwich and grabbed my hand. "We will be happy here, won't we, Ben?"

I held her hand between my own. "What a silly question," I said, with as big a smile as I could muster. The last thing I wanted her to be was unhappy, but I couldn't tell her, for certain, that – yes, we would be happy in Chanter's Hide. Avoiding the truth, at times, is better than giving it a voice. At least it's not a lie. I did tell her that Nick didn't possess a computer though, was oblivious to 'The Bank of England' and didn't know what broadband was.

"I'm a little concerned that we're totally cut off here. It's like going back to the 1930s."

She smiled. "I think that's brilliant. Chanter's Hide is so unique and unspoilt by everything that ruins the rest of the world. This is going to be a wonderful place to bring up Charlie."

"Do you not think it's weird?"

She shrugged. "It is a little out of the ordinary, I admit but, I like it."

"But we won't be able to Google anything, and what about Spotify?"

"We've both got our iPods. I've got all the music I need on there."

I sighed. "I can't get my head around it, it's bizarre."

"You'll get used to it; I know I will. We've got the telly, who needs the internet?"

"It doesn't matter if we do, we haven't got it. Do you fancy a walk, we could go up the hill, out of the village? The path leads off from the end of our road. I'll do the washing up when we get back. The rain's stopped now."

She thought about it and then said. "No, I really want to get this place straight. If I don't, it'll drive me mad. You go. You never know, you might bump into Efram on your travels."

"I know we've only been here a few days, but you've got to get outside these four walls while the weather's decent, Jan. Come on, come for a walk."

"Tomorrow, I promise," she replied. "You know what I'm like if there's clutter about. I'll be unbearable."

I could see I was fighting a losing battle. "Suit yourself." I gave her a kiss. "See you later, beautiful."

I left the cottage for the second time that day and turned in the opposite direction. I could see the path, about two hundred yards away, leading off from where West Street petered out. The sun had reappeared and made short work of drying out the ground; droplets hung on the hedgerows, waiting for their turn. The air was losing that rainy smell, that seems to incorporate the grass, flowers, sea, and summer. An aroma unlike any other. I breathed the last of it in and set off to meet the path.

The Dorset countryside is as beautiful as its coastline, a quilted wonder. Woodland accentuates the grace of the lush fields, their many shades interspersed with slabs of rapeseed. The path began with a slight incline but in the distance its climb became steeper as it reached to meet the A35. Herds of cows and sheep meandered slowly across farmland, munching on Dorset's best. I put the morning's events out of my mind as I ambled along. This afternoon I wanted to forget Chanter's Hide and its strange ways and just enjoy the scenery and the peace. I came upon blackberry bushes, heavy and un-plundered and, even though I'd just had lunch, couldn't help myself. The fruit was ripe and succulent, and I made a mental note to return with a bowl. Jan would love to make a pie or crumble out of these beauties – and I would, certainly, love to sample it. I was managing to put my worries out of my mind and really chill out for the first time since we'd arrived. The further I went, the further away, and the less important those worries became. I know it sounds corny, but I felt at peace, a tiny part of this wonderful landscape of ours. Part of our magnificent heritage. The only sounds were the occasional grumbles from the sheep and cows, the faint lapping of the sea and the cry of gulls. It was heaven on earth. Up ahead a field of Friesians chewed the cud and a stile stood between me and them. I noticed at the side was a gap with a plank of wood with a handle blocking it. A painted sign tacked to the other side of the style read – please keep dogs on leads at all times. I grabbed the handle and pulled it up. It was a door for dogs, and it made me smile. I climbed over, not being a canine, and walked slowly through the field, careful not to spook any of the beasts. Many gave me a welcoming moo. Either that, or they were complaining about me stomping through their field. I liked to think it was the former. I dodged the many cowpats, some fresh, many ancient and within minutes was faced with another stile of similar structure at the other end of the field. The next field was bright with rapeseed and the path sauntered through the middle. I climbed over and breathed in the heady, musky smell of the yellow flowers. It is an incredible aroma. I paused in the centre of the crop, a thorn amongst those scented blooms. I must have stayed there for about ten minutes, enjoying the scent and solitude. At the next stile, I climbed up and sat on the top spar, looking out over the contrast between the brilliance of the rapeseed and the black and white of the cattle. My gaze wandered to the coastline and I could see Smugglers' Rock clearly, it's craggy terrain, sharp against the blue water. On the shore looking out towards the island was the figure of a child. I could make out a calliper on one of the kid's legs and he or she was using a stick for support. Everything came flooding back as the child turned around. It was Efram's son and, as he started to hobble up the beach, I felt the same terrible sadness I'd felt on that first night in Chanter's Hide.

I sat and watched until he disappeared behind the variety of foliage between us. I dropped back to the ground and made my way back to the village. I decided to call on Efram again and I wasn't going to leave until he answered the door. The feeling that he and I were kindred spirits was becoming stronger and the need to meet his son, somehow, imperative. Before I set off, I looked up to the road and was surprised that it didn't appear to be any closer. I had crossed a few fields and thought I should be almost there. I shrugged, maybe distance is distorted over open countryside, the same way it is over water. I started back. The cows stared impassively as I hurried through their field, trying to disturb them as little as possible. The calmness I had enjoyed on the way up was gone. My emotions were in turmoil once more. I really needed to talk to someone who didn't consider Chanter's Hide, some weird, Utopian commune. Nick had said that Efram wasn't a 'Hider', in a tone that was drenched in distaste. In my hurry to get over the final stile, I caught my foot and fell headfirst, landing in an untidy heap. I got up and brushed off the dirt. I carried on, past the blackberry bushes to where the path joined West Street. I speeded up; I was on a mission.

I strode up the path to Efram's door. The curtains were no longer drawn. I knocked and waited. Almost immediately it was opened and Efram's bulky frame filled the gap.

"I wondered if you'd come," he said. "Would I be right in thinking you're not buying into the 'Chanter's Hide' dream?"

I shook my head. "And, from what I understand – neither have you."

I held out my hand. "I'm Ben, I already know your name. It seems you're not the most popular person in the village."

Efram smiled. "You could say that. You'd better come in."

I followed him in. The inside of the cottage was the complete opposite to the exterior. It was spotless and, if I wasn't mistaken, recently redecorated. A comfortable looking red, floral three-piece suite rested on polished floorboards, a large, oriental rug before the open fireplace. A small, old fashioned TV set sat on a squat table of similar age. There was a sideboard along one wall and a bookcase against another. All the furniture appeared to be circa 1950s or earlier. On the sideboard were four photographs, two showing a young Efram with a beautiful, young woman, the other two showing the pair, older, with the boy with the sad face. I guessed the woman was Efram's wife, the boy's mother.

"I begged Ted to change his will," he said, waving a hand to one of the armchairs. I sat and he plonked himself down on the sofa.

"What do you mean?" I asked him. "Change it how?"

"I asked him to leave his cottage to me. Keep it in the village. Save anyone else being imprisoned in this hell hole," he replied.

"What do you mean – imprisoned?"

"You, obviously, haven't felt the urge to pop into Bridport, or Lyme Regis – or anywhere for that matter."

"Not yet, no," I said. "Are you saying that someone tries to stop you, if you do?"

"No, nobody tries to stop you. They don't have to." He leant forward. "I'm afraid, once you take up residence in Chanter's Hide, you can never leave."

"Are you telling me we've checked into 'Hotel California'?" I saw the look of confusion on Efram's face. I waved a hand. "It's just a song," I said with a shrug. "There's a line that goes – you can check out anytime, but you can never leave. Never mind that, what do you mean, you can't leave?"

It was his turn to shrug. "You can't, that's all there is to it." He thought for a few seconds. "I saw a film once, no idea what it was called, but a bloke was driving out of this town in America – or thought he was. He passed a sign telling him he was leaving 'Yellow Rock's' – or whatever it was – city limits, then seconds later he came to the sign – 'Welcome to Yellow Rock'. He did this about half a dozen times, just going around in circles. That's pretty much how it is here. If you don't believe me, try taking a drive out somewhere."

I stared at him, wondering if I'd been wrong about him. Maybe the rest of the village didn't bother with him because he'd got a screw loose. As if reading my mind, he said.

"I can assure you; I am as sane as you are. It sounds ridiculous; it is ridiculous, but, unfortunately, true."

I thought about my walk across the fields and how the road had seemed to remain as far away after I was halfway up the hill as it was when I started.

"What about the removal men?" I asked him. "If that was the case, they'd still be driving around here now."

"Their purpose was to bring you here. You and your wife, and, if I'm not mistaken, your unborn child. They served that purpose and were allowed to return to the outside world."

"This is ludicrous," I said. "I mean, I know this place is weird, but some Utopian prison? I cannot believe that. I won't believe it."

Efram shook his head, took a deep breath. "I moved here with Peter, six years ago. I'd lost Kathy, his mother, four months prior, to lung cancer. This cottage was left to her by her aunt, I forget her name. Kathy hadn't seen her since she was a kid. She made me promise to bring Peter here and make a new start, once she'd gone. To be honest, our old place in Cheltenham was full of too many memories, anyway. And I thought the climate and sea air would be good for Peter's health. It was a done deal."

I suddenly remembered the sad faced boy and the calliper on his leg.

"I've seen your son," I told him. "Her was on the beach earlier. He has a problem with his legs?"

He nodded. "In this day and age, polio is extremely rare. There are vaccines to prevent it; I don't know if they're still administered. Peter was extremely unlucky. He contracted the disease aged four. He was very poorly for a long time. Now it's just his left leg. He will make a full recovery and, to be fair, the air down here has cured his breathing problems. As the months go on, the muscles in his leg become stronger. Soon he will be able to dispense with the calliper."

"He looks so sad," I couldn't help saying.

"He has no friends here," Efram said with a sigh. "I know you haven't been here very long, Ben. Tell me, have you seen any other children?"

It was something that hadn't crossed my mind, I had to admit. Then I felt guilty. Charlie was on his/her way and, apart from Nick and Hannah's expected sproglet, I had seen no sign of kids. Plus, if what Efram was telling me, was true – where was the school? If this place was some kind of self-contained pocket, concealed from the outside world; surely it must have its own education facilities. My mind was getting ready to explode.

"There must be other kids," I said.

He shook his head. "Afraid not."

I thought back to our first night at the pub. There were two or three couples there, close to our age, who must have had children. Every village has children. It's why we're all here – to procreate.

"So, you're telling me that, other than Peter, there isn't one single boy or girl in this village?"

He looked uncomfortable. "I'm guessing Ted didn't know about the baby," he almost whispered.

"No. I haven't seen him since I was a kid, and, from what I understand, he didn't take a great deal of interest in the rest of the family. My Dad rarely mentioned him, and he was his brother. I got the impression he was – the black sheep of the family."

Efram smiled at that. "Yes," he said. "I think he probably was. That's why we got on so well. A couple of miserable, old, cynical bastards together. I miss him dearly."

"Why did you ask if he knew about the baby?" I asked him.

"Because, if he had, he wouldn't have left the cottage to you."

I rubbed my forehead and massaged my temples. I was starting to get a headache. "I don't understand any of this," I said. "What does Charlie have to do with him leaving us the cottage?"

He took a deep breath. "There have been six pregnancies in Chanter's Hide, that I know of," he continued. "All of those women, allegedly, miscarried."

"What?"

"I don't go out much, but I see folks passing, to the pub and the shop. To visit the vicar." He spat the last two words out. "Those women were about to give birth, every single one of them. I'm no expert, but to miscarry at full term is unheard of, I imagine. There was no mention of any of them being stillborn either."

My headache was getting worse. What had we got ourselves into?

"If those women didn't suffer a miscarriage or a stillbirth. What happened to the babies?"

"I dread to think," he said softly. "But whatever it is, it has something to do with that damned island out there."

"Smugglers' Rock?"

"He takes a boat over there regularly, always at night."

"Who?" I asked.

"The, so called, vicar,"

My mind was racing. My primary thought, however, was Charlie. We'd moved to Dorset to give our child a good life, away from the temptations and degradations of city life. Admittedly, without Uncle Ted's help, that wouldn't have been possible. But here we were in, what should have been, an ideal location. I was beginning to wish I hadn't knocked Efram's door. It's often said that ignorance is bliss – maybe it is.

"In just over a month's time, my wife is due to give birth," I said to Efram. "Are you telling me something is going to happen to our baby?"

His expression said it all. "I'm sorry, Ben," he said. "So very sorry."

"Fuck you and your apologies," I said, through gritted teeth. "Whatever that bastard is doing, I'm going to stop him before Charlie is born." I grabbed his arm. "The question is – are you going to help me?"

"We have to Dad."

I turned to see Peter standing in the doorway, leaning on his stick, taking the weight of his callipered leg. He looked sadder than ever.

Efram sighed. "You know nothing about it, son."

"I used to sit behind the door and listen to you and Ted talking," he said. "Ted said, one night, that there may be a way to stop him. I heard him, Dad."

Efram glared at his son. "Ted was full of ridiculous notions," he said sharply. "And look what happened to him."

I was puzzled. "Hang on, what do you mean? Ted died of a heart attack. Apparently, he'd suffered with angina for years."

Efram looked down at the floor. "That was the 'official' cause of death," he said. "As far as Ted having angina, that's rubbish. He was as strong as an ox."

"So, how did he die?"

Efram looked up and I could see the fear and guilt in his eyes. "One night, he came around and said the vicar and his fancy piece had gone off to the island. He wanted me to go with him and break into Chanter House, see what we could find. I told him, I didn't want any part of it and if he had any sense, he'd forget the stupid idea."

"And?"

"He went anyway." He took a deep breath. "The next day, the vicar called on me. He took great pleasure in telling me that Ted had died in the night from a heart attack. As he left, he told me to take good care of Peter." He glanced at Peter and back at me. "It was a threat. He was telling me that if I had any ideas of following in Ted's footsteps, it wasn't just me I had to think about."

I realised Efram wasn't a coward, he was, merely, protecting his son. By the same token, I needed to protect my child. I needed to complete what Ted had started. I needed to find out what he meant, when he'd told Efram that there was a way of stopping Drake.

"I need to get into that house," I told him.

He shook his head. "You are so much like him," was all he said.

. "You must have some idea what's going on here," I said.

He shrugged. "All I can tell you is that Ted was convinced that Drake was a Satanist."

I almost laughed, but the expression on Efram's face stopped me. "Are you serious? Are you telling me we've really stumbled into some Dennis Wheatley novel?"

He shrugged again. "I've lived here for just under six years and I still don't know what to think. I guess black magic explains it as good as anything else."

"Efram, we're in the 21st century."

"Ted told me he'd found some sort of amulet," he continued. "I have to admit, I was worried about him. This obsession with Satanism and then this daft idea to break into the vicar's house – well, I thought he was losing it."

"Amulet?" I thought back to the box I'd found in the shed and the strange pendant that was inside. And then I remembered the book in Drake's house by Aleister Crowley and, suddenly, I knew why it had disturbed me. Crowley was alleged to be mixed up in the dark arts.

"It wasn't long after he found the old manuscripts," Efram added.

"What manuscripts?"

"I don't know. All I do know is that he was very animated about it all. That was when he first started talking about destroying the vicar's hold over this village."

"He said I needed to play my part, as well," said Peter, limping to stand in front of his father.

"He wasn't in his right mind, I've told you," snapped Efram. "What on earth do you think you can do, you're little more than a cripple."

I saw a mixture of hurt and anger explode across the boy's features. "I'm getting better," he said, his voice trembling.

Efram stood and hugged his son. "I'm sorry Peter, I didn't mean that. I just worry about you so much. You're all I have left; I can't lose you."

I watched the two of them and cursed Drake for the misery he was causing, but I couldn't stop thinking about the manuscripts.

"Do you know where Ted kept the manuscripts?" I asked Efram.

He shook his head. "He just said they were somewhere safe."

I thought about the cottage. Apart from the shed, Jan would have gone over the rest of the place, cleaning it within an inch of its life. I'm sure if there had been some old manuscripts secreted somewhere, she'd have uncovered them, and, let's face it, that's not the sort of thing you keep to yourself. There was no basement and no loft space, and I'd gone through the shed thoroughly.

"Maybe they aren't so safe anymore," I said.

"What do you mean?"

I looked from Efram to Peter and back again. "You say, the vicar came to tell you about Uncle Ted's so called 'heart attack'."

He nodded.

"I'll bet you a pound to a penny those manuscripts have now been relocated."

At least he didn't get the amulet, I thought.

A thought suddenly occurred to me. "Why, if you are so against everything that goes on here, are you allowed to stay? How do you live? You can't be part of their wonderful bartering system?"

Efram smiled but it was a sad smile. "I am an example to everybody else. We are allowed to exist in this prison and, if we didn't grow our own vegetables in the back garden, have the eggs from our two hens we would have no food at all."

"What about water and electricity?"

"Drake allows us our water and electricity but has a way of cutting off both, which he does, at least once a week – just to remind us what he could do if he wished."

"That's terrible, Efram."

The older man patted his considerable paunch. "We have potatoes, onions, cauliflower, cabbage, green beans and sweetcorn. Plus, we have a small greenhouse with tomatoes, lettuce, and cucumber. We manage well enough – don't we Peter?"

Peter smiled and nodded. "As you can see, Ben, Dad is very partial to the spuds especially."

The three of them laughed. "I'll cut down, I promise," Efram said.

I needed to get out, to have some space - to think.

"I've got to try and get my head round this," I told Efram. "I'll come back tomorrow." I stood for a few moments, looking from one to the other. "There has to be a way to turn this around." I turned and headed for the door.

NINE

As I walked home, I knew the first thing I would do. I turned into West Street and within seconds was opening the door to our new home. Although, the word 'home' didn't really seem applicable anymore. If everything Efram had said was true, it was, indeed, more like a prison, with, maybe, a death sentence hanging over our unborn child's head.

"A good walk?" Jan called from the kitchen.

I picked up the car keys from the coffee table. "Yeah, great thanks, darling. I just thought I'd take a little drive around, get my bearings."

"I'd come with you but I'm up to my elbows in flour," she said as I walked into the kitchen.

"No probs, I won't be long." I gave her a kiss, a wink and left.

I sat behind the wheel of the Range Rover, feeling apprehensive. If we were really trapped in this village and it was all down, in some way, to Drake; then the only way out was to finish what Ted had started. I put the key in the ignition and started the car. I took a deep breath, stuck it into first, took off the hand brake and was off. I was still having trouble with idea of not being able to drive out of Chanter's Hide. Well, I'll soon find out, I thought, as I turned on to High Street. I kept to twenty, not wanting to rush the inevitable. I passed Efram's place, then the pub and finally Sam Templeton's farm.

"Here goes," I muttered to myself.

After about half a mile, I came to the junction, the one we'd turned into the village from. The sign for Dorchester was still there, pointing directly ahead.

I swung the car to the left and started off towards Bridport. I was beginning to think that Efram was some sort of malicious joker, when there was a sharp bend in the road, I was sure wasn't there when we arrived. I carried on. Maybe my memory was playing tricks; after all, our journey here had been confusing, to say the least. I followed the road round until it straightened out again, trying to picture, in my mind, the map of West Dorset. However, as Chanter's Hide didn't appear on the map, the action was pointless.

"I don't believe it," I said aloud.

I was back at the T junction, the sign for Dorchester, pointing to the left. I swung the wheel left and headed towards the county town. After a few minutes I was back at the same place. I tried both routes twice more. Every time, I ended up back at that bloody junction. I slapped the steering wheel in anger and frustration. I sat there for a time, staring into space, wondering what the hell I was going to do. One thing I wouldn't, I decided, was tell Jan. I was going to sort this, God help me.

I drove slowly back into the village, mulling things over. This Satanist nonsense seemed ridiculous. I'd always considered black magic just a blanket, covering sadism, debauchery, and deviant indulgence. The idea that witches and warlocks really existed and were capable of true sorcery was just something for horror novels – surely. Since first meeting our local 'vicar', I'd known he was a wrong 'un, but a servant of the Dark Lord? But then again, why couldn't I leave this God forsaken beauty spot? How was that possible? There were so many unanswered questions since we had moved to Chanter's Hide and, apart from Uncle Ted's suspicions, I was no nearer finding answers to any of them.

I passed the pub, for the second time that day. George Porter was standing outside puffing on a sizeable pipe. It struck me as amusing. Devil and Hellfire were, apparently, the order of the day in these parts but they still adhered to the no smoking rules. I waved to the farmer but received a baleful stare in response.

It was probably all around the village by now that I was a troublemaker, not a convert to the village dream. I gave him the finger and put my foot down. I passed our street and drove to Drake's place. I decided, I needed him to know I wasn't going to let him get away with whatever he had planned for Jan and Charlie.

The gate was open when I arrived. I drove up the gravel drive, leapt out of the car and gave the silver knocker three hard raps. Within seconds Drake stood in the doorway, his Clooney smile in place. He was dressed in jeans and a plain black T shirt.

"Well Ben, this is a nice surprise. Won't you come in?" He stood back and waved a hand.

"No," I replied. "I won't. I've come for some answers."

"Ah," he said, nodding. "I understand you've been talking to Efram Stein. You really must be careful who you speak to, you know. I believe old Efram's a little mentally unstable, tends to indulge in flights of fancy." He paused, looked me directly in the eye. "Similar to your uncle Ted."

"Why can't I leave this place?" I asked him.

"Why would you want to?" His smile became sicklier and I wanted to punch him. He waved his arms around. "This is an incredible place, Ben. You could enjoy your life here, if only you'd let yourself. You're an intelligent chap. We could have many intellectual conversations and debates. I'm afraid the rest of the 'Hiders', although sterling human beings are limited cerebrally. You and I could be particularly good friends. Do you play chess?"

"I like to play all sorts of games," I said through gritted teeth. "And I don't like to lose."

He laughed and clapped his hands. "Marvellous, marvellous," he said. "I look forward to facing, what I hope, will be a worthy opponent. One thing for you to remember though." Although he was still grinning, his eyes were like steel. "I *never* lose."

I tried to stare him out, but his eyes bored into me as if he were reading my innermost thoughts. I looked away, ashamed of my weakness. He laughed.

"I'm sure you'll come around to our way of thinking, Ben." He patted me on the shoulder. "Let's face it, what other choice do you have?" He was about to close the door when he had second thoughts. "By the way, Shona finds you very attractive, and, believe me, she's an extremely passionate woman, if you get my meaning."

He closed the door and I stood there, feeling frightened and helpless. This man was pure evil, that was now obvious. Suddenly the Satanist aspect didn't appear as ludicrous as I'd first thought. Simon Drake controlled this village and everyone in it. Efram was terrified and I wasn't far behind him. As far as Peter was concerned – he was a boy with a disability. We were hardly a match for a disciple of the Dark Lord. If he was able to close off Chanter's Hide from the rest of the world, what else was he capable of?

I returned to the car and sat in the driver's seat, staring at the 'vicarage'. As if to reinforce what Drake had said, Shona appeared in one of the upstairs windows, in just her underwear. She turned to face me, smiling seductively. She reached behind, unhooked her bra, and let it fall, revealing her breasts. Despite myself, the sight aroused me. I slammed the Range Rover into gear and churned up gravel as I spun it round and headed back down the drive. The last thing I saw was Shona laughing, Drake behind her, cupping her right breast. I hurtled down the drive and out onto the road, where I jammed on the brakes. I had to calm down and think. I was shaking. I couldn't go back to Jan in this state. I banged the steering wheel in frustration. Although not one who went looking for fights, I'd always thought I could look after myself and had always been a confident sort. I had never experienced the kind of feelings that overwhelmed me now.

I took deep breaths until the shaking subsided and my head began to clear. I tried to stop my thoughts wrestling with each other, tumbling in turmoil.

"For God's sake," I said, banging the wheel again. "Come on, get a grip will you."

It was another five minutes before I got myself under control. I was a husband, about to become a father. Real men looked after their families, fought for them, if need be. I would convince Efram to help me and I would get into that bastard's house and retrieve those manuscripts. I just hoped that Uncle Ted had been right, and they contained information of how to get the better of Drake and his followers.

I restarted the car and drove home, wanting so much, to talk things over with Jan, knowing that I couldn't. If I did, she'd either be convinced I needed sectioning, or she'd be terrified out of her mind. Either way, it wouldn't help matters. I pulled up outside our cottage, leapt from the car and put on a smile, I hoped didn't look as forced as it was.

I have to say, that night was murder. The fact that I'd been a little preoccupied, shall we say, since arriving in the village helped. Otherwise Jan would be asking why I wasn't my usual happy-go-lucky self. I think I put on a reasonable show of normality and I'm sure I concealed my considerable concerns about Drake and the village pretty well. We ate another of Jan's beautifully prepared evening meals, Beef Wellington for main and Apple Tarte-Tatin for afters. It was so good that a couple of times I managed to drag my thoughts away from the vicar's grinning mush.

After dinner, I started clearing the table. As I stood, I said to Jan, "You look bushed darling, why don't you go up. I'll make sure I wash everything properly and put it all in its rightful place, don't worry."

She looked up and smiled. "I do feel pretty tired." She patted her bump. "It's this little monkey taking it out of me." She looked down. "I can't wait to see you, Charlie," she cooed.

It was like I'd been stabbed. The whole thing all came flooding back, all that Efram had said about the other pregnancies. I managed a smile, nevertheless.

"Me too," I agreed, putting my hand over hers. "Now, both of you. Get some rest. Do as Daddy says."

Her smile widened. "Yes Daddy," she said. "Come on Charlie, bedtime."

I watched her waddle up the stairs, my heart nearly breaking. At that moment, I vowed to stop Drake harming our baby, even if I died doing it. I took the dirty dishes into the kitchen and filled the sink. As I washed the plates, my mind was darting this way and that, looking for any way I could throw a spanner in the vicar's works. By the time I'd washed, dried, and put away, there was still only the one option that could, possibly, make any difference. I had to get those manuscripts. In the morning, I would call on Efram again and, hopefully, rope him in as a look-out, if nothing else. The sooner we did this, the better.

I went back into the lounge, grabbed my laptop, and sat down. I was about to throw it back on the sofa, but something made me open it up. The blue screen appeared and then the search bar came up for a few seconds, before flickering and disappearing altogether. The screen went black and I hit the 'escape' button, then 'control, alt, delete'. The screen remained dark until, gradually, from the top, it reddened slowly, dripping like blood, until the whole screen was crimson.

I watched in horror as, slowly, an image emerged, as if from out of a thick fog. As it became clearer, it was evident that it was a face. I held my breath as Simon Drake's grinning face filled the screen.

"Hello Ben," was all he could say before I slammed the laptop shut.

I was shaking, absolutely terrified. If it weren't for my conversation with Efram, I'd have thought I was going mad.

I sat there for hours, trying to figure out how I could get Jan and the baby out of this mad house, waiting for something else to happen. I had to look away from the TV, my own reflection tending to morph into Drake's.

"This is just what he wants," I mumbled to myself. "To get into your head."

I stared back at the TV, my left eye twitching in fear. "It's okay to be afraid," I said to myself. "If I wasn't, I'd be very stupid." I tried to stop my eye from twitching and was nearly there when a mouse ran across the floor and I nearly jumped out of my skin. "Jesus Christ," I almost sobbed. I was starting to lose it, and that wasn't going to do anyone any good. I sucked in air and let it out slowly, clearing my mind and reducing my heart rate. I wanted to go to sleep, to escape the nightmare for a few hours, but I was too wired. I got up and started to pace, but then thought I might wake Jan. I let myself out into the mild chill of a late summer night, the moon, a huge light overhead, casting vague, silvery shadows. "A killing moon," I thought, and shivered. I made my way to the beach, hoping to bump into Efram. I was in dire need of a friend. As I turned towards the coast, I looked back and saw only darkness. All lights in the cottages, even the pub, were out. For the first time in my life I felt totally alone. I walked slowly down to the sea, a ball of uncontrollable fear. What was I supposed to do against the evil that nestled here in Chanter's Hide, against the vicar from hell? This was a situation, not sorted by a quick jab and a swinging right hook. I was out of my depth, floundering in the unknown. As I approached the beach, I heard voices, one of which, I couldn't mistake.

"Not long now," I heard Drake say. "We'll hurry them along. He'll soon be in our midst."

"Do you think Ebbrell will be a problem?" Shona asked him.

Drake laughed. "How can Ben be a problem? A mild irritant, maybe." He paused. "No, I'm sure he'll come around. He has two choices – join us or join the children. He's just going through the protector/provider thing at the moment. He's not stupid, he'll soon realise the second choice is no choice at all. Come on, we have things to do."

I heard some rustling sounds and then a 'splosh' as if someone or something had been dropped into the water. I edged forward and saw Drake and Shona floating across to 'Smugglers' Rock' in a rowing boat, Shona at the oars.

I realised I didn't need a lookout. This was the opportunity I'd been looking for.

I walked back up the lane towards the vicarage, my heart beating like a Royal Tattoo, my legs shaking. I focused on Jan and Charlie, telling myself that I was doing this for them, which I was. I needed to keep Jan's face in my mind's eye and visualise Charlie's future, away from this graveyard. I turned into the driveway and tried to keep the sound of gravel under my shoes to a minimum, even though I knew Drake and Shona were otherwise engaged.

By the time I reached the front door, I was one step up from a nervous wreck. I stood there for a full five minutes, eyes closed, regulating my breathing.

"You have to do this," I told myself.

TEN

I gripped the doorknob and prayed. I took a deep breath and turned it. The door swung inwards silently. I suppose I shouldn't have been surprised; after all, what did Drake have to fear from the villagers he controlled. The house was in darkness, the only light, the glimmer of the moon trying to penetrate it through the open door. I took out my phone, turned on the flashlight and closed the door behind me. It was then I realised that I'd been holding my breath and let it out slowly, my heart still racing. Breaking and entering wasn't something I was familiar with, although, technically, there had been no breaking. I wondered if you could be charged with just entering. I shook my head and set my mind back to the job in hand. I crept up the hallway, wondering where to look first. I thought back to our dinner date and remembered a large oak desk in the library, where we were supposed to have our aperitifs. I shone the torch onto the wooden panelling along the hall until the beam reached the library door. I turned the handle and entered. The curtains were drawn back, and the moonlight cast an eerie glow about the room. Once more I felt as if I was in one of those old Hammer horror films, where Dracula lurked in the next room, about to wake and rise from his coffin. I shivered and padded over to the desk. As I expected, the drawers were all unlocked. In one I found several charcoal drawings, six of which were of a naked Shona. They were very explicit but also exceptionally good. The rest were drawings of Chanter's Hide from a variety of viewpoints. It seemed that Drake was a talented artist. The last sketch was disturbing, to say the least. It showed a figure with the body of a well-endowed male and the head of a goat. Something sprang into my mind, probably from one of the Dennis Wheatley novels I'd read, about the 'Goat of Mendes'. I think it was either supposed to be the Devil or one of his henchmen. I wished I were more knowledgeable in the black arts, not that it would have done me much good, I guess. The rest of the drawers held documents listing weird transactions between Drake and the villagers. Had I more time, I would have liked to study them in more detail. As it was, I was here for one reason and one reason only.

I left the library, no further forward. The rest of the downstairs rooms revealed nothing of importance either. A plush lounge, the dining room, the kitchen, and conservatory were, more or less, what you would expect.

I returned to the staircase, to the left of the entrance. It swept up in a crimson curve, the moonlight dribbling through the front door's picture window. I've never been one for feelings of foreboding before but, as I put my foot on the first stair, I have no other way of describing my emotions. I climbed slowly, gripping the mahogany banister tightly. My fight or flight responses at that precise moment were veering ever closer to flight.

"Come on, you have to do this," I said to myself, my throat dry as sand. I urged myself on, focusing on Jan's beautiful face and the bump she was carrying. I reached the landing, legs trembling, heart beating like Keith Moon on speed. I took a deep breath and stepped up to the door to my right. It was slightly ajar. I pushed it and it swung in without a sound. I almost turned and ran, but, instead, I held my ground and mumbled a prayer to a God I'd never really believed in.

The head moved slowly from side to side, its tongue darting in and out. The yellow eyes held me; the hood extended. I was face to face with a King Cobra. It was coiled on the desk in front of me, the head and top third of the body erect, the forked tongue flicking in my direction. I had never had much experience of snakes and had never been bothered either way, but this thing was huge. It began to hiss, its hood lengthening and I felt warm urine soaking my pants and jeans. I stared into those eyes, unable to move, my lips trembling as I prayed. I saw it draw its head back to strike and let out a terrified whimper and closed my eyes, resigned to my fate.

"I'm sorry, so sorry," I wept like a child, wondering where the brave, protective husband and father had gone. I stood there, waiting for the Cobra's fangs to latch on and debilitate me with its venom. "Oh God, please help me," I whispered.

Suddenly I was grabbed from behind and slung to my left, where I went sprawling on the landing floor. "Stay there," I heard Efram snarl. I looked up to see him throw a jar of some kind into the room. I heard the snake scream in my head, and Efram slumped to the floor beside me.

I slung my arms around him and hugged him tight, tears running down my face.

"I…thought I was d…dead," I managed between sobs. "What the fuck was that?"

"I think it was one of Drake's familiars," he mumbled. "According to Ted these Satanists have certain species they can control or conjure up. I'm not too sure how it works."

"What did you throw at it?"

His face fell and the tears ran freely over his cheeks. "Kathy's ashes," he croaked. "They were all I possessed that were blessed."

I felt his pain. "Oh Efram, I'm so sorry." I hugged him tighter, letting his tears fall on my shoulder. He pulled away. "Let's just do what we came to do, shall we," he said flatly, drying his eyes.

I nodded and we both got to our feet. I peered into the study. The cobra was gone. I rushed over to the other side of the desk and yanked opened the top left-hand drawer. It was empty. I grabbed the handle on the right and pulled. It was locked. "For Christ's sake," I hissed. "The bastard's locked. The manuscript has to be in there."

"Get out of the way, "said Efram, rushing forward, reaching inside his jacket. I moved back and he pulled out a wheel iron. He jammed the end in the gap between the desk and the drawer and pushed down. The front of the drawer splintered and fell to the floor. I shone my flashlight in and reached forward. I pulled out a thin sheaf of foolscap sheets and was just about to peruse them, when Efram punched my shoulder. "Look at them later," he snapped. "Let's get out of here."

We ran down the stairs and out of the front door. I couldn't get the cobra out of my mind, its fangs, the hypnotic eyes. I imagined the venom seeping into my bloodstream as my skin was pierced. If it hadn't been for Efram, I would probably be a dead man now. Plus, he'd sacrificed his wife's ashes to save my life. This was a man I'd known for a couple of days.

We reached the road, and both glanced, automatically, towards the beach. There was no sign of Drake. We both breathed a huge sigh of relief.

"Come on, we'll go back to my place and see if Ted was right about those pages you've got," Efram said.

I put my hand on his arm. "I can never thank you enough," I said, unable to stop the tears. "What you did in there....well....it breaks my heart."

He looked at his feet, to hide his emotion, but his voice betrayed him. "It was the right thing to do," he replied shakily. "Kathy would have wanted me to do it."

"It was all you had left of her," I said softly.

"I still have my memories," he almost whispered. He coughed, took out a handkerchief and blew his nose. "Now, let's go, before the bastard comes back."

It suddenly occurred to me that my visit to Drake's house hadn't been planned and Efram could have had no idea I was there.

"How did you know I was in there? Don't get me wrong, I'm glad you did."

"I couldn't stop thinking about you and Jan and your baby. Peter kept on as well, saying we had to do something. It was his idea to take his Mum's ashes. I know they make numerous trips to that bloody rock, so I thought I'd try my luck. I was on the beach when they went off to the island. It wasn't until I was in there, I realised I wasn't alone. I thought he might have left one of his followers on guard. I nearly left, but I thought I'd try and see who it was. It seems, two great minds think alike."

"And I'm grateful they do," I said, as we hurried down the drive.

Walking back to Efram's, a thought occurred to me. "Can he see through that snake's eyes?"

He shrugged. "I guess so. In any case, he won't have to look far for suspects if he can't, will he?"

I nodded. "I suppose not. Unless, of course, there are other rebels in the village."

"I can assure you there aren't," said Efram confidently. "They're all just sheep, hanging on his every word; terrified of him."

"What do you think he'll do, when he gets back?"

"Put it this way; we're going to be off his Christmas card list, that's for sure."

Despite ourselves, and what was now hanging over our heads, we both burst out laughing. Minutes later we were going through Efram's front door. Peter was waiting, chewing his fingernails.

"Where have you been, Dad?" He asked anxiously.

Efram held up his hand. "Calm down son. We've paid Mr. Drake a visit."

"What? Did you get the manuscript?"

"We did."

"Have you read it?"

"We haven't really had the time," I said. "One thing I will tell you though – your dad is a hero. Tonight, he saved my life."

Efram looked down at his feet. "It was your mum that saved his life. Not me."

Peter hobbled up to his dad and they hugged, both unable to hide their grief.

"It worked then," said Peter, into his father's shoulder.

"Yes, I'm sorry son."

Peter pulled back. "We're all in this together – including Mum."

I had never felt so humble, but also, so blessed to have these two on my side. The question was – would we, and the manuscript, be enough to stop Drake?

"Look," I said. "It's late. I'll take this home and go through it tomorrow. We're all knackered and if Jan wakes up, she'll think I've been abducted by aliens." I gave Efram a hug of my own. "I can't thank you enough," I whispered in his ear. "I'm grateful to have you as a friend and an ally, as, I'm sure, Ted was."

He put his hands on my shoulders and eased me back, until he was looking into my eyes. "I let Ted down, and I'll always regret that" he said. "We can't live in fear anymore. We're the good guys.......aren't we?"

I nodded. "You know we are."

"We've got God on our side," said Peter. "Although, if you listen to Bob Dylan, so did Hitler. I believe He lets us get on with things unless we call him."

"Who? Bob Dylan or God?" I was feeling more myself. "In any case, what's a young lad like you doing listening to Bob Dylan?"

"He loves Bob Dylan," Efram said. "I was never really a fan. I prefer Abba."

I couldn't stop a smile. I have nothing against Abba, they produced some wonderful pop records but to compare them to his Bobness was like comparing a Rolls Royce to a Volvo. No disrespect to Abba or Volvo, of course.

I left them to their slumber, although I didn't think any of us would sleep particularly well that night. I'd stuck the manuscript under my T shirt, as if it were a bullet-proof vest and, as I walked home, I started to yawn. I really was exhausted. I suppose being confronted by a huge, metaphysical snake that was ready to sink its fangs into your throat does that to a person. I looked at my watch and saw it was almost two in the morning. It had been a long night. As I turned left into our street, I couldn't help looking towards the beach and the road towards Drake's place, wondering if he and Shona were back yet. There was a slight chill in the air, a sign that summertime didn't go on forever, even in Dorset. I looked up into the night sky, the stars, diamonds, and crystal in their black, velvet, unpolluted home. This was a beautiful part of England, without a doubt. Why did it have to be spoilt by the likes of Drake?

I reached our cottage, let myself in quietly and settled myself down on the sofa. The urine had dried, and I made a mental note to throw my jeans into the linen bin in the morning. I didn't want to wake Jan; she and Charlie needed their sleep. Although I was burnt out, I couldn't stop thinking about that cobra. I still couldn't believe that Efram had thrown his wife's ashes to save me. I lay there for about two hours before I finally dropped off. My sleep was troubled, to say the least, but relatively normal until Drake and Shona barged their way in. They cavorted, copulated, grinned at me, whilst giving me the thumbs down and slicing their hands across their throats. I tried so hard to wake up but was unable to. I finally managed to escape the arms of Morpheus in a sweat, with Drake telling me that what I'd stolen from him would do me no good. As my eyes opened, I could still hear his mocking laughter. I looked at my watch – it was six thirty. The manuscript was on the floor by my side. I picked it up, tried to read it and groaned.

It was Greek to me. It resembled some kind of weird hieroglyphics. I kept staring at the first page, all hope I'd managed to sustain, dashed. I, suddenly, felt empty and totally powerless. Efram and I had risked our lives for nothing. Drake had won and there was nothing we could do to stop whatever plans he had in place bearing fruit. Although I knew it would be pointless, I took out my phone, photographed the text and uploaded it to the laptop. If there was internet access, I might have been able to find an app that translated the text into English. I wondered why I kept picking the damned computer up in the first place.

I nearly threw it across the room. I refrained and, instead, buried my head in my hands and wept. Whatever I had done in my life, I'd always been in charge. Sure, I'd made some bad decisions – but they were my decisions, made by me. Not by some power mad devil worshipper. I'd had some low points in my life, but this had gone beyond the cocked hat. I shut the laptop in case our unfriendly vicar decided to make another of his gloating appearances. I was devastated. I'd pinned all my hopes on that manuscript, and it had let me down. And I wondered why Drake had bothered to steal it from Ted, if there was nothing my uncle could do with it. It didn't make any sense. My head was full of weary resignation and my heart wasn't far behind.

"You're not a quitter," I told myself and, to be fair, I never had been. The more I ran the situation through my head though, the fewer options seemed available to me. The only clear thing that was that I would die trying to save Jan and Charlie from the vicar and his evil commune. I just couldn't see how my death was going to help either of them.

I heard Jan padding across the landing to the toilet and looked at my watch again. I was amazed to see it was now nearly 7.30. I took the manuscript and slipped out of the back door and crept down to the shed. I secreted it my man cave and returned to the cottage.

Jan had just reached the bottom of the stairs as I walked back through the back door.

"What happened to you last night?" she asked.

"Oh, I couldn't sleep. I went for a walk," I tried for a smile and failed. "I stayed on the couch, didn't want to wake you two."

"Are you all right, Ben? You don't look too good."

I accepted the way out. "No, I'm feeling a bit iffy. Do you mind if I go back to bed for a couple of hours?"

"'Course I don't. Do you want me to bring you anything?"

I shook my head. "No darling. I just need to get some rest. I'll be fine."

With that I slouched upstairs. Knowing what I now knew, I couldn't face Jan, without saying anything. And that was out of the question.

I took a quick shower first. I felt incredibly dirty, especially after having peed my pants. I stood under the dribble, trying to clear my head. I still couldn't understand why Drake would bother stealing Ted's manuscript when it was obvious that it was useless. The more I thought about it, the more confused I became. The bogus vicar was not a stupid man, not by any stretch of the imagination, and not the type to waste his time and energy on fruitless tasks. And why have his pet cobra guard it. It was ridiculous. I got out of the shower, towelled myself down and padded back to the bedroom. When I'd told Jan I needed to rest, that had been the furthest thing from my mind. There was no way I could even consider sleep. Now, however, I felt exhausted – drained, and the idea of closing my eyes was turning into a need. I slipped beneath the duvet and listened to Jan singing along softly to her iPod as she made her breakfast. I smiled and vowed to record her before I got any deeper into this mess. In the past, the choice of funeral songs or pieces of music had been discussed, with friends and acquaintances and I could never come up with anything for mine. Now I knew. When my coffin slid towards the flames, I wanted Jan's dulcet tones sending me on my way. My eyes closed, the trauma of the previous night taking its toll, my brain needing to shut down before it blew a gasket. I floated away to Jan singing the Mamas and Papas old hit 'California Dreamin'. She loved sixties' music, especially the American bands. Over the years she'd introduced me to The Lovin' Spoonful, The Byrds, The Beach Boys, The Mamas and Papas and many more. Although not as enthusiastic as her, I saw why these groups had stood the test of time. As Denny Doherty's vocals mixed with Jan's, backed by Cass Elliot and Michelle Philips, I sank deeper, like a stone in quicksand. I welcomed the oblivion as the fanciful fathoms of slumber drowned me in waves of somnolence. That's a flowery way of saying – I slept – and I dreamt.

I was at a concert, my arms above my head, swinging, a lighter in my hand. The music was indistinguishable, the band invisible, but I could feel the beat of the bass drum in my chest, an additional heartbeat. As I swayed, I was aware of my fellow concert goers slowly disappearing, until I was on my own in a huge venue, the noise in my head dissipating, my mouth becoming drier. I turned away, glad of the peace. The venue became a forest, the trees painted with frost. I could see my breath and feel the chill in my bones. I felt lost and overwhelmed, a stranger ignored and discounted, banished. I curled myself into a ball and tried to shut out the impending surge I knew was coming.

'The ankh,' a soft whisper in the dark. I saw a shadowy figure being dragged away, through the fog. I had time to see the face of Ted before it was replaced with the evil, grinning features of Simon Drake. I may have been mistaken, but I thought I detected a hint of consternation.

I awoke with a start, a strange sense of optimism coursing through my veins.

I had just been given a sign; I was sure of it.

ELEVEN

I looked at the clock and was surprised to see it was just past midday, the sun shining unimpeded through the bedroom window. Even if I'd drawn the curtains, their flimsiness wouldn't have been much of a match for its brilliance. It was another beautiful, late summer's day in Chanter's Hide. I lay there wondering about my dream. Now I was fully awake, my earlier hope was dwindling as reality kicked in. The talisman I'd found in the shed contained an ankh, but I'd scrutinised it closely when I first discovered it and was certain it had no markings of any description. The dream was probably just a conglomeration of stuff in my head, as I drifted off. There was still something lingering though, some niggling trace of belief. I needed to re-examine Ted's old pendant, at least. The more I thought about it, the more I was convinced that it meant something. Whether that was just wishful thinking, coupled with desperation, I didn't know. I guessed I'd soon find out.

I slid out of bed and got dressed. My stomach was growling, a spot of brunch wouldn't go amiss before I paid another visit to my man cave. Or maybe, that was just another ploy to put off the inevitable. Nevertheless, I needed something in my stomach. I slid my feet into a pair of flip-flops and made my way downstairs. I'd expected to find Jan in the kitchen, but she wasn't there. I called her name, panic beginning to set in and then I heard her voice. She was in the front garden, talking to someone. I heard her laugh and a chill ran through me when it was followed by the unmistakable sound of Drake's guffaw. I bolted for the door, a mixture of anger and fear forming a heavy ball in my stomach.

"What do you want?" I blurted as I stumbled into the sunlight.

Jan's expression was one of extreme embarrassment coupled with shock. Drake smiled and gave me a wink as Jan turned her death stare on me.

"Simon was just telling me a funny story," she said through gritted teeth. "About his first day as vicar of Chanter's Hide."

I mentally cursed myself for my outburst and tried to rectify the situation.

"Sorry vicar," I said, shaking my head. "I didn't sleep very well last night. I'd just nodded off and was having a terrible dream. Jan was being abducted by a serial killer. I guess I was still half asleep. Please – accept my apologies."

Jan's features softened and she came over and slid her arm through mine.

"It must have been a real nightmare," Drake said with a grin. "A man must always protect his woman."

"Indeed." I put my arm around Jan. "And that's exactly what I intend to do. Anyway, nice to see you again, vicar; have a nice day."

"You too, Ben," The look he gave me indicated that I wouldn't be enjoying too many more. He turned his attention back to Jan. "You take care, Mum. Look after little Charlie."

As he walked away, I turned to Jan. "I never mentioned Charlie to him, did you?"

She shook her head. "I don't remember doing, but I suppose I must have."

I took her in my arms and laid my head on top of hers. "I love you," I said. "Don't ever forget that."

She pulled her head away and looked into my tear-filled eyes. "What is it, Ben? What's the matter? You haven't been yourself since we moved here. Are you missing London?"

I wanted to tell her everything. My heart was practically breaking. I wiped away the tears. "You know me," I said. "If I don't get enough sleep, I get weird and emotional. I'll be fine."

"You don't regret coming here, do you?" she asked.

"Of course not, darling," I lied. "How could I regret moving to such an idyllic place. Charlie's going to love it." I pulled her back into my arms and kissed the top of her head, choking back more tears. She hugged me back and I closed my eyes, wanting to stay like this forever. But I knew that wasn't possible.

"I'd better get back to the garden," I said. "It's not going to clear itself." I gave her a wink and walked back into the cottage before I said something I shouldn't.

I went through the lounge and kitchen and out of the back door. I suddenly realised I'd been holding my breath again and let it out in ragged gasp. I gazed at the stumps and partially weeded mess but saw nothing. My mind was elsewhere. I walked slowly down to the shed, my steps echoing the apprehension I felt. I had never experienced such feelings of hopelessness before, never known the desolation that now consumed me. My earlier optimistic leanings had disappeared. I was in a blue funk. I opened the shed door and breathed in the stale and musty smell of Ted's shrine. I took out the manuscript again, hoping it had translated itself into English overnight. It hadn't. I opened the metal box and took out the pendant. I scrutinised it for a good ten minutes but found nothing. I cursed Uncle Ted for giving me false hope. I threw the ankh onto the useless pages and buried my head in my arms. I stayed like that for a while, my mind racing. I'd always prided myself in being a rather good problem solver, but, now, I was lost. I lifted my head and looked through the dusty, shed window seeing a prison instead of a cottage. Anger flared and I was about to dash the ankh and manuscript to the floor when the sun caught the eye of the ankh and I gasped. The pendant translated the script. It lost its hieroglyphic structure and became text. Unfortunately, it appeared to be Latin. I'd been educated at a grammar school and for the first year we'd been forced to learn Latin. Apart from – amo, amas, amat, though, I was lost. It had been a few years and I hadn't taken much notice at the time. I could never see the point in learning Latin, unless you intended becoming a doctor or horticulturist, which I didn't.

I yearned for the internet to come to my aid. I could certainly have found a site that translated Latin to English. I wondered if the power of the pendant might extend to things of a technological nature. I was clutching at straws but, nevertheless, went into the cottage. I could hear Jan singing away upstairs. She'd obviously managed to sort the ground floor to her satisfaction and now she'd turned her attention to higher places.

I picked up the laptop and fired it up. Once I'd signed in, I brought the pendant close to the screen, hoping to see the Wi-Fi symbol burst into life. Deep in my gut, however, was a heavy ball of pessimism. So far Drake had managed to thwart me at every turn. I stared at the laptop, willing it to show a connection, even if it was weak. I imagined the vicar's bloody, beady eye in the sky, watching my every move. I must have sat there for a good ten minutes. I stood up and would have thrown the useless computer across the room if Jan wasn't upstairs. That would be the icing on the cake, proving I'd really lost my marbles. Instead I lay it back on the coffee table and went back to the shed.

It was becoming more and more obvious that I was totally out of my depth and powerless to stop Drake taking my child, doing whatever he liked with Jan and disposing of me. I toyed with the idea of taking him up on his offer and joining his evil band. It would save Jan and I, but we'd still lose Charlie. I berated myself for even entertaining the notion.

I tried not to but couldn't help wallowing in self-pity. Normally I would have been disgusted with myself for such behaviour, but now, I couldn't see any future. I decided there and then, when it came to it and we were about to lose everything, I would end it. I would not let that bastard take my child and defile my wife. I wondered if Efram possessed a gun. I scooped up the manuscript and ankh and left the shed. I needed to see a friendly face and to ask him the dreaded question. He would understand, I was sure of that.

I went through the kitchen; Jan was still singing her heart out upstairs. There was no point in disturbing her. I let myself out of the cottage quietly and headed for Efram's place. I wondered why I had brought the manuscript and Ted's pendant and realised I was still clutching at that last straw. Maybe Efram was a secret linguist.

He answered the door almost immediately. I didn't have to say anything, he could tell by the look on my face.

"I gather it's no help," he said, his expression matching mine.

"Unless you're fluid in Latin – no."

"You'd better come in." He stepped aside and I entered his cottage. Peter was sat in one of the armchairs reading 'The Lord of the Rings'.

"Pity Gandalf can't pay Chanter's Hide a visit," I said to him. "We could do with a wizard on our team."

"What about the manuscript?"

I shook my head. "Unless you can read Latin?"

"There has to be a way," he said. "Good always triumphs over evil."

"I'm afraid real life very rarely mirrors the novels we read and films we watch, Peter. You just have to look around the world to see that. Evil is everywhere, slowly smothering what good there is left." I slumped down onto the sofa. Efram took the other armchair.

"Peter's right," he said. "We can't just give up."

"I handed him the manuscript. "If you've got any bright ideas, I'm all ears."

He looked down at the strange language crawling like a demented spider over the pages. "This isn't Latin – is it?"

"Oh no." I took the ankh out of my pocket. "That translates it into Latin." I gave him the pendant. "Hold the aperture over the text."

"That's weird," he muttered.

"We've got to be realistic; we have no chance." I looked at Efram and gave him a sad smile. "At least you won't lose your child. You just carry on living your life the way you have been doing, keeping yourself to yourself."

"I doubt if Drake is going to allow that to happen now. He knows we're in cahoots." He shook his head. "No, I'm afraid Peter and I will go the same way as Ted. We're in this together – win or lose."

"I'm sorry," I said softly. "If I hadn't have approached you in the first place, you wouldn't be in danger now."

"No point crying over spilt milk," Peter said with a grin. "Can I have a look at the manuscript?"

Efram got up and handed it to his son. " It might as well be in Russian," he said.

Peter took the pages and jumped in his chair. "Wow," he said. "Can you get a shock off paper? Give me the pendant, Dad."

Efram handed it over and as Peter took it, he sat up straight, his eyes bright, both hands trembling.

"You okay Peter?" Efram asked him.

I lay my hand on Efram's arm and shook my head. "Wait," I whispered.

The ankh began to glow in Peter's hand, a shaft of light moving on the manuscript. Suddenly the boy began to speak – in Latin. The light moved over the lines of text, the pages turning by themselves as the beam reached the bottom of each sheet. I could tell Efram was becoming agitated as he watched his son, trance like, reciting the ancient text.

"I think this is meant to be," I whispered to him fervently.

He glanced at me and then stared back at his son. "You'd better be right," he said.

Peter rattled his way through the manuscript. When the beam of light hit the last part, the pendant lost its vitality and dropped into his lap. For a few seconds he remained bolt upright, eyes wide. Then he blinked, lowered the pages, and looked at his Father. "With faith comes power," he said. "Those that have risen will be cast back down."

Efram grabbed his son's shoulders. "Peter?" He said softly, looking into the boy's eyes, their faces mere inches apart.

"I'm fine Dad," Peter said, and smiled. "We will win this battle."

"What did you see in the text?" I asked him.

"The manuscript and the pendant are just keys," he explained. "But there is one more."

It was then I realised how elated I had been feeling. Peter's last statement brought me back down to earth. "What do you mean? There is nothing else in Ted's cottage, I've searched it from top to bottom."

"The last key is on the island," he said.

"The island? Do you mean 'Smugglers' Rock'? Efram asked.

Peter nodded.

"And what is it, this final key? What will it unlock?" I demanded, feeling that this was just another wild goose chase, engineered, somehow, by Drake.

"As to what it is, I'm not too sure," Peter replied. "What it unlocks – is the force that separates Heaven from Hell. A power that may be used by either."

"So, does Drake have access to this...key...or whatever it is?"

Peter sighed. "He knows of its existence and has been searching for it. So far, it remains hidden. Simply, we have to find it before he does."

"Oh, that's all right then," I said sarcastically. "We're practically home and dry."

"Steady on Ben," Efram said sternly. "There's no need to take your frustration out on Peter. At least we do have a chance now."

"So, what do we do? Swim over to the bloody island?"

Efram looked at Peter and they exchanged a smile. "Hopefully, we won't need to," he said.

"What? You've got a boat?"

TWELVE

"It's yet to touch the water," said Efram. " I bought it just before we moved to Chanter's Hide. I thought that once Peter was more mobile, we could get out and get some sea air, maybe do a bit of fishing."

"Why didn't you?"

"Drake warned us off; telling me about the strong under-currents flowing between here and the rock and how unpredictable they were. At that time, I had no reason to doubt him."

"What sort of boat are we talking about," I asked him.

"It's only a dinghy," he replied. "But it's pretty robust."

"And it has a pair of oars," Peter added.

"A dinghy?"

"It might be a bit of a squeeze, but I reckon, for the short distance to the island, we wouldn't be too cramped," Efram said.

"Dad, we'll be fine," said Peter. "We can do this."

"What if we don't find the last key before Drake?" I asked.

"What if, what if, what if," Peter blurted in frustration. " Would you rather sit back and let Drake do his worst?"

I looked at Peter and then at Efram. "You should be very proud of your son, Efram," I said. "He has courage and common sense in spades."

Efram beamed. "He takes after his Mother," he said with a sad smile.

Peter sighed. "When you two have stopped with all the schmaltzy stuff?"

"Okay," I said. "First off, we'd better make sure this dinghy is still seaworthy and hasn't perished, or whatever rubber does."

"It'll be fine, "Efram said. "The problem is going to be, making sure that Drake is not out there when we are. We could do with some sort of diversionary tactic."

"How about your wife?" Peter asked.

"What about my wife?" I said sharply.

Efram picked up on his son's stream of thought. "Can't you get Jan to invite him and his fancy piece to dinner? Return the compliment, so to speak."

"That's all well and good," I said. "But I think both she and him would expect me to be there as well, don't you?"

That seemed to take the wind out of their sails until Peter's face lit up.

"Have you still got that step ladder?" He asked his Dad.

"Yes, it's lying along the back fence. Why?"

"Is your bedroom window big enough for you to get out of?" He asked me.

"I guess so," I said. "At a push."

Peter had a glint in his eye. "If we play this right, "he said. "We may be able to pull the wool over our friendly vicar's eyes."

"Come on then, clever dick, let us into your cunning, little plan," I said.

He grinned. "It's simple really. Your wife invites Drake and his whore for...."

"Peter!" Efram exclaimed.

Peter looked at his Dad sheepishly. "Sorry Dad, but she is."

"Well, I'd prefer it if you didn't use words like that. I'm sure your mother wouldn't have approved."

Peter nodded, looking suitably ashamed. "So, Jan invites Drake and Shona (he emphasised the woman's name) to dinner," he continued.

"What if he declines the offer?" I asked.

Efram snorted. "As if that's going to happen. He thinks he's got you by the short ones, he'll come, just to gloat and wind you up. He plans on convincing your wife that you're a suitable case for treatment."

"Mmmm, I guess that's it, in a nutshell," I said. "Go on Peter, I'm all ears."

"Well – halfway through dinner, you feign illness and tell them you need to go and lie down for a while. Drake will think you're just trying to get away from his taunts and will just love telling Jan how worried he is about you."

"He's right," said Efram. "This is just a little game to Drake, something to pass the time. Watching you fall apart is what it's all about."

I sighed. "And, so far, I've been giving him, more or less, what he wants."

"That's about to change," Peter said, his expression suddenly stern. "We're going to wipe that stupid, evil grin off his face."

"Or die trying," I said.

"Come on, Ben; we have no choice. If we do nothing, we dead anyway; and so is your unborn child. We're doing this, yes?"

I looked at the two of them, the determination etched into their features, and felt ashamed. "I'll get Jan to invite them tomorrow night. She'll love preparing a meal for her favourite vicar. I just wish she could see what an evil bastard he actually is."

"She will," Efram said. "Soon, she'll see him for the devil he really is."

"Before we get ahead of ourselves, shouldn't we check out the dinghy?" I said. "Without it, we don't have a plan."

Efram shook his head. "It's still in a sealed bag in the shed. It will be fine, oh ye of little faith."

"Ben's right Dad, with all the weird things the vicar appears to be able to do around here, we'd better make sure it hasn't turned into a..... bucket or something."

"Okay, follow me."

We went out into the back garden, which was a total contrast to the front, I have to say. It was a vegetable grower's paradise, rows, and rows of shoots in various stages of growth. Efram unlocked his shed and I was impressed. It was as tidy as it could possibly be. I let out an involuntary gasp.

"I like things tidy," he said, as if reading my mind. "I just hate gardening for the sake of it. I'm fine with the veg but Kathy was the gardener." He took a plastic bag off a shelf on his left. "Here it is, good as new."

It looked as if he had just bought it from the shop. Surely it wasn't possible for Drake to be aware of all his parishioners' possessions. I crossed my fingers.

"Have you got a pump?"

Efram bent down and straightened up with a red foot pump in his hand. "The adaptor for the dinghy is in the bag, I think."

"Well, I hope it is, because we've got no chance of popping into Bridport for one, if it isn't," I pointed out.

Peter grabbed the bag from his Dad and tore it open. A small, yellow plastic spout fell to the floor. "There it is," he said excitedly. "We'd better pump it up, make sure there are no holes."

"I told you, it hasn't been out of the bag, son," Efram said again.

"But what if it was faulty when you bought it," I said. "It could have been sat out here all these years and it's a dud."

Efram shook his head. "I bought it from a reputable store in Dorchester, it'll be fine."

I couldn't shake the thought that Drake was watching everything we were doing; waiting for us to pump the bugger up and then, somehow, mentally puncture it. After all I'd seen and experienced so far, it wasn't that far-fetched.

"Let's just do it," I said. "The bloody suspense is killing me. "

Peter lay the dinghy flat, smoothing out the edges and, I must admit, it was in pristine condition. Efram picked up the adaptor and fitted it to the foot pump's corded tube. I held my breath as he pulled the plug out of the dinghy's air hole and inserted the adaptor. He took the safety clip off the foot pump, put it on the path and started to pump. Slowly the craft began to become the shape it was meant to be. I listened for the hiss of escaping air but heard nothing. After a minute or so, Efram removed the pump and reinserted the plug. "There you go – what did I tell you?"

I let out my breath slowly, not wanting to disturb the optimistic atmosphere that had suddenly enveloped the three of us. We stood, still as statues, looking at the dinghy.

"It seems we have finally been given a slice of good luck," I said quietly.

Peter was grinning and Efram's expression said, 'I told you so'. I was just relieved. "Shall we let it......." I stopped mid-sentence as the hiss of escaping air confronted us. "Oh Jesus, no," I said with a groan.

Peter was on his knees running his hands over the dinghy. "It's here," he exclaimed. " Just a tiny hole. Dad, have we still got that puncture repair kit?"

"Er, yeah, I think so." He dove back into the shed. I was distraught. This was Drake's work. I could just see him watching us, laughing like a drain.

Peter looked up at me. "It's just a pinprick, we'll fix it. This is nothing to do with him."

"How do you know?" I said. "How can you possibly know?"

He shrugged. "I don't know, I just do. Have faith Ben, we can do this."

We waited with bated breath whilst Efram rummaged about in his shed. If he couldn't find it, we were sunk – literally. I suddenly realised how futile some peoples' lives must seem, when life never gives them a break. A line from an old blues song came to mind, originally recorded by Albert King, I think – If it wasn't for bad luck, I wouldn't have any luck at all. At that specific moment, that was how I was feeling. I was growing more and more impatient and dreading Efram emerging, empty handed.

"Is it there?" I almost pleaded.

It seemed like an eternity before he finally ducked his head under the door's lintel. He was smiling broadly, holding up a small, yellow, oval shaped tin.

"You worry too much, "he said, clapping me on the back.

"Never mind that," I retorted. "Open the bloody tin and make sure what we need's in there."

He struggled with the lid for a few seconds before it popped up. He reached in and brought out a piece of chalk, a sheet of six patches with one missing and a tube of glue.

"How old is that?" I asked, imagining the patches to be perished and the glue to have lost its adhesive quality completely.

"Probably three of four years, but it will okay, stop worrying."

"That's easy for you to say, your unborn child's life isn't on the line," I muttered.

"For Christ's sake, pull yourself together, Ben. I've told you – we're in this together. Win or lose, the consequences will be the same for Peter and me, as for you, Jan and Charlie."

"He's right, Ben," Peter said. "And no matter what is thrown at us, we knock it for six and carry on."

Despite myself, I had to admire his turn of phrase. Yet again I felt like the weak link in this fragile chain.

I sighed. "I've got to man up, haven't I?"

They both nodded. Efram grabbed hold of my shoulders. "Ted used to say you were a feisty bugger."

"I guess I used to be," I said. "That was before I had others to think of. I'm just so scared of screwing this up."

"Well, get that feistiness back. It's the only way we're going to beat this bastard."

"One for all and all for one," said Peter, with a grin, holding up his hand for a high five. We obliged, the action lightening the moment.

"Now, let's repair this puncture and get ourselves seaworthy, like true musketeers." Efram suggested.

"Just call me Aramis," I said, trying on a smile for size.

I couldn't leave until the puncture had been repaired and tested. I still wasn't convinced that this was nothing to do with Drake. It was only when the dinghy had been pumped up and let down three times that I began to regain a smidgeon of my earlier optimism.

Efram looked at me and shook his head. "Go home, Ben. Everything's good this end. Go and talk to Jan, get this dinner party sorted out."

Peter gripped my forearm and looked into my eyes. "You really need to start being more positive, Ben. We're going to get him." He dropped his voice so that his father couldn't hear. "We're going to blow the bastard out of the water."

I couldn't help smiling. Here was a young kid, still suffering from the remnants of polio, eager to take on the vicar and his moll; and here was I – one step up from a nervous wreck. I was beginning to wonder how ashamed I could feel. I held out my arms and said something I'd never said before, in fact cringed, when it had been said by others. "Group hug."

Peter was there in a flash, although Efram seemed to be a little reluctant. I must admit, that, up until that point, other than my dad, I'd never wanted to hug another male. At this moment, it had passed from desire to need.

After a few seconds Efram pulled himself free. "Now go home," he repeated, clearly uncomfortable with hugging other men, himself. Peter peeled himself away. "Yeah, let's get this show on the road," he said, with a glint in his eye.

I nodded. "I'm all over it." I managed another smile, before turning to go.

"Wait," said Peter. "Aren't you forgetting something?"

I stopped and looked at him. "What?"

"Duh – ladder."

"I'll get it," said Efram.

"I'd forget my head if it was loose," I said to Peter. "Especially at the moment."

Seconds later Efram was back with a wooden, two section ladder, easily long enough to reach the bedroom window. "There you go, Ben. Good luck."

"Cheers Efram, I think I'm going to need it. If everything goes to plan, I'll meet you at the beach as near to nine as I can manage." I took the ladder from him and manoeuvred it through the front door. I made my way up the path attempting as hard as I could to walk the walk. My determined stride probably looked more like one of Monty Python's silly walks, but at least I was trying.

Luckily, I never bumped into any of the dreaded 'Hiders', on the way home. I couldn't muster any enthusiasm to lie about why I was carrying a step ladder; I wasn't in the mood, to say the least. I went over Peter's plan in my head and, although it seemed quite simple, there were two factors that were plaguing me.

First off, I was crap at lying, especially when it was premeditated. Secondly, I was convinced that Drake would see straight through my deceit. I berated myself yet again for negativity. "Come on, you spineless git," I said to myself. "You can do this."

THIRTEEN

It was almost five thirty when I reached our cottage. I stopped and listened. I couldn't hear Jan, so I made my way quickly around to the back.

"Where have you been? And why are you carrying a ladder?"

I almost swore. Jan was getting the washing off the line.

"Oh, I popped round to Efram's," I replied, trying, frantically, to think of a reason for being in possession of a ladder.

"And the ladder?"

It came to me in a blinding flash, as if sent from above. "Old Efram was saying how badly the guttering round here gets clogged up with dead leaves. He reckoned he was pestering Ted to get them cleared out before we got any serious rain. That's before the old bugger popped his clogs, of course. Ted, that is, not Efram." I was starting to ramble. I gave her the best smile I could muster.

"So, he offered to lend me his ladder."

"He sounds like a nice man, "she said. "You'll have to introduce us."

She carried on un-pegging the towels and tea towels and I felt so guilty. It seemed to me that all I'd done since arriving in this God forsaken place was lie to my wife. Maybe I wasn't as bad at it as I thought. Before then, I couldn't recollect telling her any significant untruths. I may have fibbed about how many pints I'd had at the pub, once or twice, but didn't every bloke?

"Do you want to go and wash your hands, dinner's almost ready," she said, picking up the linen basket.

"Here, I'll carry that," I said, taking it from her, thinking – here goes then. "Talking of dinner, I was wondering about asking Simon and Shona. You know, repay the compliment, so to speak."

"Oh," she said, her surprise evident. "I'd really like that. That's a really nice thought, Ben."

"How about tomorrow night?"

"It's a bit short notice, don't you think? They might already have plans. What's the hurry?"

"I didn't behave very well when we went to theirs, I'd just like to make amends as soon as possible, that all," I lied again.

"Well, if they're free, I'm up for it."

"I'll pop and see Simon first thing in the morning," I said, with a grin. "I'm sure they'll jump at the chance."

"Just don't go pressurising him," she urged.

"Don't worry, I won't." I laid the ladder under the kitchen window, kissed Jan on the forehead and went in to wash my hands, ready for dinner. First part of the plan activated, I thought. Part two should be a breeze. Drake would take any opportunity to make me squirm. He would be sure that Jan had insisted on the return invite and that I was dreading it. He would certainly be right about the second part.

The rest of the evening was a trial. I had no real appetite but managed to force half a plateful of Jan's Beef Bourguignon down.

"What's wrong?" She asked. "That's one of your favourites."

I gave her a wan smile. "Just feel a bit off colour, darling. Don't worry it's nothing to do with your marvellous culinary skills."

"I should hope not," she said sharply, and then, with a look of concern. "Maybe we should put off Simon's and Shona's dinner invitation, if you're not feeling up to it."

I suddenly realized that my nervous tension – no, change that to – downright fear – was hampering the plan a little.

"It's probably too much sun, something like that. I'll be fine tomorrow."

"If you're still feeling iffy in the morning, you're not going round there, okay?"

I nodded. "Yes, Ma'am."

"I don't suppose you're up for sherry trifle, either then?"

"Oh, I love your sherry trifle," I said. "Keep it in the fridge, I won't see it go to waste, I promise you."

Jan reached over and put her hand on mine. "Why don't you go up to bed. I'll clear up here, probably watch one of the 'Orange is the New Black' episodes and be up later. Just go and sleep it off, whatever it is."

"But I was going to do the washing up."

She stood up and pointed to the stairs. "Go."

"Well, if you don't mind. I do feel bushed, I don't know why."

"Go," she repeated.

I must admit, I was relieved. Sitting, watching TV had much less appeal to me tonight than usual and, at the best of times, it had very little. The thought of sitting there with Jan, whilst the whole, sorry predicament chased its tail through my head, was not a pleasant one. I would be better off upstairs, out of the way. I didn't envisage getting much sleep tonight. In fact, until this was over, sleep would be, probably, very much in short supply.

I kissed Jan goodnight and trudged up to bed. As I climbed the stairs, I tried to plan my actions for the following day. First thing would be a full recovery for me, with plenty of assurance that I would be fine for the upcoming dinner. Second would be the visit to my favourite vicar, where I intended to be subservient and apologetic, trying to convince him that I was seriously rethinking the situation. I may even hint to him that I had been feeling a bit off the previous evening but was fine now and looking forward to making amends for my previously, unacceptable behaviour. I just hoped that he wouldn't be able to see through it. If everything went to plan, my upset stomach would make a reappearance halfway through dinner and I'd make my excuses and go up to the bedroom. I made a mental note to remember to put the ladder in position before Drake and his bitch arrived.

I lay awake, listening to the muffled sounds of 'Orange is the New Black', with the occasional laugh and gasp from Jan. It was going to be a long night. Mentally, I moved our plan forward, beginning with me back on the street and heading for the beach. With the community so tightly knitted and every other inhabitant of Chanter's Hide under Drake's evil thumb, it would be good if I weren't spotted on the way there and the three of us weren't seen launching the dinghy. If we were, it would be sure to get back to the vicar and alarm bells would ring. Next, I started to wonder if Peter had any idea what we were looking for on Smugglers' Rock and, indeed, where we might find it. The more I thought about our mission, the more hopeless it seemed to be. First, I was going to try and con some sort of Satanist, whose powers were, from what I'd already witnessed, quite considerable. Second, three of us were going to attempt to sail out to the island in an old dinghy, one that could easily turn into a colander, on the way over. And, third, we going to search for some unknown item that could be anywhere. It was a plot from one of the poorly written novels, I used to reject without a moment's hesitation, in a previous life. After all that, however, I had to try. I had to hope that Peter was right, and that Uncle Ted hadn't been a mad, old trout. There was no other option.

About an hour and a half later, Jan came up. I pretended to be asleep and she climbed in beside me, plumped up her pillows, let out a satisfied sigh and settled down. Within minutes she was snoring softly, and I couldn't help envying her. I seemed to glance at the clock every twenty minutes or so, trying not to toss and turn too much. As it was, Jan let out a few sleepy moans, as if I were disturbing her. The last time I remember seeing the time it was four fifty. I must have dropped into a troubled sleep after that.

Jan got out of bed just after seven and I opened my eyes. They were sore and gritty, and I felt exhausted. I sat up.

"'Morning you, how are you feeling today?" Jan asked, with a broad, expectant smile. She had always been a morning person. Me, on the other hand, even at the best of times, had always been the reverse. I returned her smile, rubbed my eyes. "I feel fine, darling. A good night's sleep has done me a power of good," I lied, once again. I couldn't tell her I felt like shit and was terrified of the day and night ahead.

"I'll go and get breakfast going, I'm starving, I don't know about you?" She said, leaving the bedroom.

"You bet, "I called after her. If I could get this lead ball out of my stomach, maybe I'd be able to eat a little breakfast. Maybe.

I ambled to the shower and stood under the drizzle for a time, hoping the water would revive me. It didn't. I shaved, cleaned my teeth, going through the motions automatically. Today, I thought, could be do or die.

By the time I sat down for breakfast, I'd managed to calm myself a tad. I'd decided I was, after all, a man and not a mouse, and it was time I started to behave as such. Even so, I passed on cereals and waited until Jan had eaten her Weetabix, sipping orange juice. I told her I was saving myself for dinner and asked if she had decided on a menu.

"Of course, I have," she said, spooning up the last of the milk and cereal. "Organisation's my middle name, Remember?"

I nodded. "Indeed." I waited for her to wax lyrical about her courses, but she took her bowl to the sink and busied herself with the eggs.

"Well?" I prompted.

She turned her head and smiled. "You're going to have to wait and see," she said coyly.

If I'm honest, I was glad I didn't have to ooh and aah over her dishes, most of which I wouldn't touch anyway. I was thankful for small mercies.

The aroma of grilled bacon filled the kitchen as she opened the oven. It was waiting patiently with sausages and mushrooms, for the fried eggs to arrive.

As Jan dished up, I confess the lead in my stomach shrunk, leaving a little room. I wasn't ravenous but I could definitely eat something.

"That smells wonderful," I said enthusiastically.

"It's only a fry up," said Jan.

"Yeah, but you can't beat bacon and eggs," I replied.

"Well, strictly speaking, you can beat eggs. I do it all the time."

I grinned. "Ho, ho."

I picked up my knife and fork and dived in. If I could eat half of it, I would be happy. Once I began munching, however, I didn't stop until I'd cleared my plate. I sat back and patted my belly, feeling pleased with myself.

"Beautiful, as usual," I sighed.

"Good. Toast?"

"No thank you darling, that will do nicely. I'll wait for the mystery menu. Any clues?"

She waved her finger at me. "Everything comes to he who waits," she laughed.

And everybody gets what they deserve, I thought, hoping it was true. I looked at my watch. It was ten to nine. "I think I'll mosey over to Simon's and deliver the dinner invitation," I said. "I'll tell him you're keeping the details a heavily guarded secret."

"Just don't put any pressure on him. Okay?"

I gave her a semblance of a boy scout salute. "No, ma'am."

"Go on, get out," she said, shaking her head and chuckling.

When I hit the day's heat, my legs became wobbly and the breakfast threatened to reappear. I realised how much I was dreading the next part of the plan.

I confess, the walk to Drake's place could have been a lot quicker. After the wobbliness subsided, my legs took on a leaden feel. My stomach was still trying desperately to hold on to the bacon and eggs it had been thoughtlessly bombarded with. My mouth kept filling with water, and I was continuously swallowing. I was metres away from the vicar's driveway when I had to give up and let nature take its course. I threw up in the hedge, heaving until I was dry retching. Luckily, I had a handkerchief in my pocket. One of the old school. I was able to wipe my mouth and eyes and blow my nose before going any further. I thought that hoofing up might have made me feel better – I was wrong.

I took a deep breath and set off up the drive. My attempt at a determined stride failed miserably, the lead in my calves putting the mockers on anything other than a shuffle. Although it was only a matter of seconds, it seemed like an eternity before I was standing at the front door, heart beating like a plethora of hammers. I was giving myself a good talking to, building up to ringing the bell, when the door opened. Drake was wearing a navy T shirt and stone coloured shorts and looked almost as shocked as I did.

"Well, this is a surprise, Ben." He looked me up and down. "Are you alright, you look as though you've just seen a ghost?" He asked, the usual, evil glint in his eye.

I swallowed, as more bile tried to escape.

"Cat got your tongue?" He added.

"I... I'm here to apologise for my previous behaviour," I said croakily. "And to invite Shona and yourself to dinner tonight."

He almost took a step back. "That's a turn up," he said, grinning. "Has the little woman put pressure on you?"

I knew if I tried to smile it would appear sickly and false, so I remained po-faced. "No, actually it was my idea. I think we got off on the wrong foot, I'd like to start again, if we can."

It was obvious he was suspicious. From being his arch enemy to trying to buddy up with him was a massive step. After all, he wasn't stupid, and he knew I wasn't either.

"Someone entered my house and stole something last night, Ben. You wouldn't know anything about that, would you?"

'Oh shit,' I thought. Our foray into breaking and entering had slipped my mind with all the excitement and planning. I nearly lost it and admitted everything but managed to keep it together – just. I returned Drake's gaze, thinking about Jan and Charlie and what would happen if I crumbled now.

"Why should I? What was stolen?" I tried to look concerned but probably managed constipated instead.

"Oh, it's not important, forget it. What's brought on the change of heart?"

I shrugged. "If you can't beat 'em, join 'em." I did, this time, give him a sickly smile.

"If you're trying to pull a fast one, I'll find out," he said through gritted teeth. "You know that, don't you, Ben?"

I held up my hands. "Look – I know when I'm beaten. Will you come? Jan's really looking forward to it."

I never realised a smile could hold so much malice. "Shall we say eight?"

"Eight would be good. Look forward to seeing you later, Simon."

I turned and fought the urge to run down the drive.

"If you're messing with me, you know I'll crush you," he called after me.

I held up a hand in acknowledgement but kept on walking. I couldn't believe I'd forgotten about pissing my pants as a giant cobra readied itself to end my life; but mainly – how Efram had saved me. It seemed like betrayal. I apologised mentally to my new friend. Step two, however, had been accomplished. In the past, on occasions, I'd professed to hate somebody or other. I realised now, that had been false. It was only now; I knew what real hatred felt like. I needed a little moral support, so I texted Jan and told her it was on for tonight and I was just going to call in and see Efram on the way back. A message came on the screen telling me it hadn't been possible to send the text. Of course not, I thought. She would already be in the kitchen cutting and chopping, preparing a meal fit for a king. Certainly, too good for Drake and his slut.

As I reached Efram's house, he was just coming out of the front door.

His expression was one of expectation. "How's it coming along?" He asked.

I ushered him back into the house. It wouldn't do for Drake to spot us together after I had just told him I was about to become, in effect, a 'Hider'. Yet another village idiot.

When the front door was shut, Efram asked. "Is the deed done?"

At the sound of his father's voice, Peter joined us. "Hi Ben, is he coming?"

I let out a heavy sigh and nodded. "Tonight."

"What did you say to him?" Efram asked me.

"Can you believe I forgot all about last night and the manuscript?"

"Oh God, yes. What did he say?" Efram asked.

I relayed the conversation I'd had with the vicar and Efram slapped me on the back. "Good man, well done."

"Yeah, but the worst bit is yet to come," I said with a sigh.

"All you've got to say is you don't feel well, and slouch off upstairs," Peter said. "It'll be a doddle."

"Have you got any of those disgusting sweets left?" Efram asked his son.

"Toxic waste? Yeah, good idea Dad." Peter hobbled out of the lounge up to his bedroom.

"If these things don't make you want to throw up, nothing will," said Efram.

A few minutes later Peter returned with a small bag. "I've only got three left," he said apologetically.

"Have you got one of the green ones, you gave me?"

"You bet," Peter replied with a grin. "Dad was green after having one of these. He was nearly sick for real."

Efram shook his head and pulled a face. "I've never tasted anything like it, and I don't want to again."

I looked from one to the other. "Great," I said.

"It's just what you need," Efram continued. "Take my word for it – you will look bilious."

Peter handed me the 'sweet'. "Just hide it under your napkin or something, pop it in when you're ready, and Bob's your uncle."

I took it off him, eyeing it suspiciously. "I wish he had been."

FOURTEEN

Efram asked me if I would like a tea or coffee and I nodded eagerly, rather like a drowning man clutching at a sliver of flotsam. I knew I was putting off the inevitable, but I figured a little procrastination, at this point, was acceptable.

While his father was in the kitchen, I asked Peter if the pendant had provided him with any more info on the remaining key.

"'Fraid not, "he said. "Maybe when we get to the island, it'll.... sort of......show me something else." He held his hands up in a 'don't ask me' gesture.

I nodded, returning to the fear and apprehension that was addling my brain and turning my stomach into a cement mixer. I didn't think I'd have any need for Peter's disgusting lump of 'confectionary'; I was doing fine on my own.

"Anybody would be nervous," the boy said softly, as if reading my mind. "I would be and, although my Dad would say he wasn't, he would be too."

I smiled. "Thank you, Peter. I wish I could say that helps but, if I did, I'd be lying."

"Lying about what?" Efram returned with a tray of mugs. He handed me a coffee and Peter, a tea.

I shook my head. "Nothing really," I replied. "Your son was trying to pour a little oil on my troubled waters, that's all."

"Look, Ben, I'll be honest, I wouldn't want to be in your shoes tonight," he continued. "But, if I was, I'd look at my options."

A bit more flotsam floated by. "What options?" I asked excitedly.

Efram pulled a face. "That's what I mean – you don't have any."

The flotsam sailed out of sight. "For a moment, I thought I'd missed something," I said morosely.

"I suppose Peter and I could go over to the island, while you keep Drake happy."

It's coming back, I thought.

"No. It has to be all three of us," Peter said, with a firm nod of his head. "It won't work, otherwise."

"Will you stop getting my hopes up," I said sharply.

Peter glared at his Dad.

"I wasn't," Efram said bluntly. He looked sheepish. "I was just looking for another option for you. I guess there isn't one."

I sipped my coffee, my insides churning even more. I wished Efram would keep his mouth shut. He wouldn't.

"If Jan and Charlie weren't involved, how would you feel?" he asked me.

I thought about it for a minute or two. "If my wife and baby were safe, elsewhere," I said. "I'd throw everything I've got at the evil bastard."

"That is the way you have to look at it," he said. "Because, if you don't, you'll be handing them over to him."

Realisation crashed over me in a torrent. I'd been looking at this the wrong way all along. Thinking that by not upsetting the apple cart, I was keeping Jan and Charlie safe. The truth was, while Drake was breathing, they would never be safe. I had to fight. I stood and shook Efram's hand. "Why didn't you say that to me before? Let's destroy the sadistic piece of shit."

I left Efram's feeling positive. We were going into battle, he, I and Peter, fighting for our families. Throughout my life, although I hadn't committed any serious crime, I had never considered myself – good. I had been a reasonable enough sort of person, I guess, but never gone out of my way to do a good deed. There were much better people in this world than me, let's put it that way. In this scenario however, I was a member of the diminutive 'Team Good', the definite underdog in this conflict. Earlier today, that thought would have chipped away more of the paltry self-belief I had left. Now, it spurred me on. As I reached my garden gate, my stride was determined. It was just pat 10.45 as I opened the front door.

"I'm back," I called.

"Well, don't get in my way," came the response. Jan's head popped around the door frame, her hair scraped back, anchored with an elastic band, her face smeared with flour, her expression determined.

"What did they say?"

"They jumped at the chance. By the way, you look gorgeous," I said with a grin.

"And you're a liar. Now go and do something.... that......keeps you out of my way, all right?"

"Whatever you say, my sweet. Just remember – it's only the vicar."

"Not helpful," she said.

"Okay, I'll leave you to it," I said holding up my hands. "I'll carry on with the back garden."

"Mmmm," was all I got.

I went back out of the front door and down the side passage to the garden. I didn't fancy going through a war zone. I went to the shed, pulled out an old flowerpot and sat for a while, feeling the sun's vibrancy on my skin. I took out Peter's obnoxious sweet and sniffed it. It didn't smell disgusting, in fact, there was little odour at all. The proof of the pudding, however, is in the eating. I made a mental note not to forget to put the ladder in place before I went back in.

In the unlikely event of Jan coming into the garden and seeing it, I already had a response ready. Tomorrow I was going to clear out the guttering and, maybe, clean the windows as well.

I decided to clear more of the undergrowth and retrieved my trusty scythe. A couple of hours hard labour would do me a power of good. I took off my shirt and starting swinging; unable to shake the sight of Drake's head tumbling from his body with every cut. One day, in the not too distant future, that would, hopefully, become a reality. I swung harder, relishing the pull on my muscles. I was feeling more alive than I had done since arriving in this Hell hole. I watched the seventieth vicar's head fall to the ground and then looked up to the sky.

"If you're really there, big man, we could do with a little help," I said softly. I'd never been a religious sort, probably veering towards agnostic rather than atheist. I guess. I thought there was something inside each of us, the seed of our individuality that, maybe floated off somewhere when we shuffled off this mortal coil. But as far as God was concerned, I'd never been a believer.

Just after one, Jan called me in for lunch. I was rather disappointed to be met by a tuna and cucumber sandwich and a banana. Apparently, I failed to hide my chagrin.

"I thought a light lunch would be best today," she said. "Don't worry you'll be able to make up for it tonight."

"No – no, that's fine," I said with a smile, disgusted with my lack of appreciation. "I'd rather save myself for whatever delights you have in store for us. It smells wonderful, by the way."

"It should, I've put my heart and soul into this meal."

"I'll bet," I said, hating the fact that she'd gone to so much trouble for the vicar and his whore. If she only knew what was really going on here, in this, supposedly, idyllic village. Hopefully, when it was all over, she'd see him for what he really was – the spawn of the devil.

We both munched away, mine gone in a couple of minutes. I didn't realise how hungry I was.

"Good God," Jan exclaimed. "What a pig!"

I grinned and tried, unsuccessfully, to suppress a burp. "Gardening's hungry work," I said.

She suddenly looked concerned. "You know, you've been weird altogether, since we moved here, with your mood swings and the fluctuations in your appetite."

"Nothing to worry about, my sweet," I lied again. "Must be the change of water. Everything will settle down soon, just wait and see."

"I hope so. What are you going to do now, because I still have stuff to do in here and I don't want you under my feet?"

I held up my hands. "No probs, I know my place. I'll go and do a bit more in the garden and work up more of an appetite for tonight."

"Don't go getting sunstroke or anything, it's pretty hot out there now."

I gave her the thumbs up. "I'll be fine." Her mention of sunstroke, however, had put ideas into my head. What better excuse to use tonight? That way I wouldn't need Peter's toxic waste; just say I was feeling a bit lightheaded and needed to lie down. Jan would jump on it and berate me for ignoring her earlier. I would apologise profusely to her and our guests and, regretfully, take my leave.

I left her to her preparations, went back to my scythe and imagination. I was feeling better than I had in ages and was looking forward to our trip to the island. Whatever happened, Drake was going to have a fight on his hands, I was going to make sure of it. I couldn't believe how negative I'd been through all of this. How did I expect to defeat him with an attitude like that? I applauded Efram for making me see things differently. I started swinging again and Drake's head began rolling once more.

If I do say so myself, I put in a damned good afternoon's work. By the end of it, I had enough cut grass to make a couple of good-sized bales, and the garden was less of a jungle and more of a hacked-up mess. It would look fine when I'd put the fine touches to it. I was surveying my good work when Jan popped her head out.

"I'm going to grab a shower," she said, and then, as she took in my efforts, she added. "It's a lot shorter, I'll give you that, Percy. By the way, it's nearly six thirty."

I looked at my watch in disbelief. I'd been hacking off vicar's heads for nearly five hours. It's true, time flies when you're enjoying yourself.

"I'll finish off out here, then jump in when you're done," I told her.

She moved her attention from the garden to me. "My God, you've caught the sun, you look like a beetroot."

"I love you too," I replied, with a grin. This couldn't be going any better, I thought. I could feel sunstroke coming on already.

"Yeah, I think I got a bit carried away. I didn't realise I'd been out here for so long. Don't worry, I'll rub some 'After Sun' on."

Jan disappeared back into the house, making herself beautiful for Drake more important than my sunburn, obviously. I put my gear back in the shed and stretched my aching back. Hours bent double, scything away takes its toll, believe me. I waited until I heard Jan turn on the shower, Then I went to the back wall where I'd lain Efram's ladder. It was well maintained, and the sections slid easily and quietly. I placed it gently just under the bedroom window, jumped on the bottom rung a few times, making sure it was safe on the dry ground. The last thing I wanted, was to go from top to bottom quicker than I intended. I would be hard pushed to explain why I was lying in a heap in the back garden, after going to bed with suspected sunstroke. Especially with an extended ladder lying by my side. I think Drake would definitely smell a rat. I went up to the top and back a couple of times and was satisfied with its firmness. I heard the shower go off and Jan called out. "It's all yours."

By the time I reached the bedroom, she was sat in front of the dressing table mirror, in her bath robe, drying her hair.

"The aroma in that kitchen is intoxicating," I said to her, walking over and putting my hands on her shoulders. I bent and kissed her neck. "And so are you," I added.

She giggled. "Sometimes, you're so sweet," she murmured. "Now go and get in that shower – you stink."

"Whatever you say Ma'am," I said. I kissed the top of her head, only just avoiding another swing of the hairdryer. I took off my sweaty clothes, dropped them in the linen bin and hit the shower. Soon I would have to give my first acting performance but now, I was relishing the thought, although still very apprehensive.

By eight fifteen, we were both ready and both nervous, for different reasons, obviously. Jan was worried, unnecessarily, that her dinner wouldn't pass muster, and I was feeling first night jitters. Jan looked radiant, her maternity dress a subtle shade of blue. Tiny white flowers meandered randomly, the neckline bordering on low cut, but tasteful. After seeing Drake's 'Dark Side of The Moon' T shirt, I had dug out one of my own, depicting another 'Floyd' classic – 'The Wall'. I wore this over a pair of black chinos. Maybe we could pretend to chat about music for a while, before I made my excuses and went off in search of something that would, hopefully, contribute to his demise.

"You look gorgeous," I told Jan.

"Huge, more like it," she said with a sigh. "I'll be glad when Charlie decides to make an appearance."

"Not too long now, darling," I said, feeling for her. It must be hell on earth for women in the latter stages of pregnancy in weather like this.

"I haven't seen that T shirt for a while, didn't Simon have a......."

I cut her short. "Yeah, 'Dark Side of The Moon'," I said. "Maybe we have more in common than I thought."

She smiled. "I'm sure you have, Ben. You just need to give him a chance, that's all."

"Yeah," I said, smiling back. "We just got off on the wrong foot." I held up my hands. "I know – my fault entirely."

"Let's just enjoy the evening," she said.

"I can't wait," I lied. "Especially for the wonders you'll have conjured up for us."

She suddenly looked terrified. "I hope they like it. They might hate it. Oh Ben, I'm so worried. What if they don't like what I've cooked, I'll be mortified."

I took her in my arms. "Your cooking is legendary," I said soothingly. "It'll knock spots off what Shona dished up, believe me."

"But she cooked a beautiful meal. She......"

I put my index finger over her lips. "Ssshhh. Yours will be better. Now stop worrying."

She took a couple of deep breaths. "I just want it to be a nice evening."

Lying, by this time, seemed to be second nature. "And it will be. Now, come on, pull yourself together, they'll be here in a few minutes."

A sharp knock at the door heralded their early arrival. Jan went into panic mode again. "They're here now, they're early. Oh my God."

"Calm down woman, it'll be fine, I promise. I'll go and let them in, you take a few more deep breaths."

I kissed her cheek and went to the door. I had to take on some extra oxygen myself before I opened the door. Show time, I thought.

FIFTEEN

The breath I'd drawn in was taken away again. I was both disgusted and ashamed of myself. Shona smiled, and I couldn't take my eyes off her. A snug, low cut, short, red dress clung to her curves as if was part of her. Her nipples stood proudly, her black hair flowing in lustrous waves to her shoulders. Her dark eyes appraised me as I ogled her, the guilt building second by miserable second. I had never seen a more beautiful and sexier woman in all my life. I hated myself for every debauched thought that raced through my sinful mind.

"She scrubs up well, as they say - eh, Ben," said Drake enjoying my discomfort. He dropped his voice to a whisper. "If you really have turned over a new leaf, she's more than willing to – how shall I put it – accommodate you, in your time of need. Although pregnant women are said to bloom, in my opinion, they become rather frumpy looking."

Drake wore a midnight blue shirt, open at the neck. It hung loosely over a pair of white denims. It took all my willpower to drag my gaze from Shona and look into his bright blue, roguish eyes. I wanted to punch him. With every fibre of my being, I wanted to beat him bloody, until nothing was left of that supercilious grin. However, I had to play the game – for the time being. I comforted myself that, soon, he would be getting all that he deserved. I managed a smile.

'You look amazing,' I mouthed at Shona and she grinned. She lifted her hand and ran her index finger slowly down the side of my face and winked. She moved closer until her breasts were almost pressing against my chest. Her perfume was intoxicating.

"Aren't you going to invite us in, Ben?" She asked.

I stepped back, nearly stumbling. "Come in, come in. We've both been looking forward to this so much."

As they passed me, Shona playfully squeezed my buttock. I am more than ashamed to admit that this part of the pretence was not too difficult to pull off. Although she was nothing but a whore, she was a spectacularly good looking one.

Jan met them at the kitchen door and led them to the dining room, a room we had yet to use. All our meals had, so far, been eaten in the kitchen.

"I'm so glad you could come at such short notice. Would you like a glass of wine? Ben?"

"Red or white? "I asked, getting into my role.

"Red for me please Ben," Shona said sexily, her eyes looking me up and down.

"Simon?"

"I'll have red as well, Ben, please."

I went off to the kitchen, wishing I had some arsenic I could add. I had already decided to eat Jan's starter before beginning my act. I just hoped I would be convincing enough to fool Drake and Shona.

I poured two glasses of Merlot, a glass of Chardonnay for myself and an orange juice for Jan. She had already put the silver tray she kept for special occasions on the kitchen table. If it had been up to me, I'd have used the battered, old wicker thing we'd found in the cupboard; one of the few reminders left by Uncle Ted. Still, I had a part to play here. Jan was still playing things close to her chest. They were various platters and plates on the table, covered in foil.

The oven was on low, obviously keeping something hot. I shrugged; after the starter it was immaterial, I'd be on my way to Smugglers' Rock with my new, best buddies, searching for the final key. So far, we had the pendant and the manuscript, and I wondered what the last piece of the puzzle could be. Maybe it would be a blazing scimitar and I could do, for real, what I'd been doing, mentally, in the back garden all afternoon. I put the glasses on the tray and re-joined the party. As I entered the room, Drake was just finishing some anecdote or other and Jan was practically in hysterics. He had his hand on her shoulder and I wanted to smash his face in. Shona turned, at my entrance, smiled, licked her lips, and pushed up her breasts seductively. I smiled back, made sure Jan wasn't watching, then tipped her the wink.

"Here we go folks," I said, with a lightness I didn't feel. "Sets of dentures, or, should I say, aperitifs."

Jan looked at me, still smiling and shook her head. "The old ones aren't always the best, Ben, I'm afraid."

"Ah, leave him be, Jan," said Drake, matching her smile. "It's good to see him in such good humour."

Jan nodded. "Yes, Simon, I agree. He's been a bit under the weather since we moved here. It is good to see him back on form. Even if his jokes are awful."

I joined in the ensuing laughter. Jan ushered us to the table, and we sat. I was opposite Shona, with Jan's seat by my side and Drake was facing her, as it should be, if you were having good friends for dinner. Jan went to the kitchen.

"Nice T shirt, by the way, Ben," said Shona. "I take it you're a fan of the depressing group."

Simon did a bit of tutting. "I'm afraid Shona doesn't appreciate the power and beauty of Pink Floyd's music, like we do, Ben."

"I guess you either love them or hate them," I said.

Shona reached over and put her hand over mine. "Maybe you can convince me," she said, looking into my eyes.

I have to say my jaw was starting to ache with the stress of trying to keep a smile on my face. "Maybe I can," I said, pulling my hand away just before Jan re-entered the room, carrying three plates, like a professional waitress. She placed the first before Shona, then Drake, then me. It was salmon and asparagus in a watercress sauce, and it smelled delicious.

"Please – start," she said. "Don't wait for me. I'll only be a minute anyway."

I looked at the other two and shrugged. "Dig in guys," I said. It was food of the Gods and I was so sorry it would be the only course I would eat tonight.

I had meant to make my move halfway through the course, but it was so good I couldn't. I put my knife and fork down and sighed.

"That was sublime, darling."

Drake nodded, dabbing his mouth with a napkin. "Absolutely to die for," he agreed.

Shona smeared the last morsel of salmon with the remains of the sauce and popped it into her mouth. She smiled as she chewed, swallowed, licked her lips, and made the vote unanimous. "You must give me the recipe for that sauce, Jan. It was out of this world."

Jan was beaming. "Of course, Shona. I'm just relieved you liked it."

"Liked is an understatement, believe me, Jan," said Drake. "It was a culinary masterpiece."

Jan gathered up the plates, blushing, but over the moon. She had been told so many times, over the years, how good a cook she was, I couldn't understand why she was always so nervous at dinner parties.

"The main won't be long," she said. "Ben, pour Simon and Shona more wine."

I saluted and did as I was told. I stood to pour the wine and made a point of slumping back in my chair awkwardly.

"Are you alright, Ben?" Shona asked, with a good impression of genuine concern.

I rubbed my eyes and took a deep breath. "Just feeling a bit lightheaded, all of a sudden. "I blinked, as if I were having difficulty focusing. "I was working in the garden all afternoon." I gave them a weak smile. "Jan warned me. I meant to put some 'after sun' cream on, but, as usual, I forgot."

Drake scrutinised me and I felt as though I were at an audition for a major role.

"You do look a little peaky," he said. "The sun, around Chanter's Hide can be deceptive, especially if there is breeze and some low cloud. You could have a touch of sunstroke, you know."

Tom Hanks eat your heart out, I thought. I couldn't believe this was going so well. Maybe, when this was all over, I ought to give R.A.D.A. a call. Just then

Jan re-entered, carrying two large dishes of roast potatoes and mixed veg. I stood again, making out that I was going to give her a hand, stumbled and fell back on my chair.

"What on earth's the matter, Ben?" she asked, putting the dishes down easily.

Her concern *was* genuine.

"I think he may have a touch of sunstroke," Drake offered.

Her expression changed from one of anxiety to one of accusation. "I told you," she said sharply.

I looked at her, wearing my best apologetic, sickly smile. "I know, I was stupid." I rubbed my eyes again. "Things are starting to look fuzzy." I shivered. "I think I need to lie down."

Jan shook her head. I could see she was fuming, but it couldn't be helped. She came over to me. "Come on, I'll help you upstairs."

"Sorry everyone," I said apologetically. I let Jan lead me upstairs, flopped onto the bed.

"I really am so sorry, sweetheart, "I said. "I think I need to sleep."

I closed my eyes and listened as she stomped down the stairs. I couldn't help congratulating myself on a superb performance. Now to the next step.

I gave it a good fifteen minutes, listening to the muffled conversation below. Jan had put on one of her Joni Mitchell albums, as a bit of background music, and I welcomed the additional sound cover. I sat up on the bed, took off the shoes I'd been wearing and placed them under the bed, where I'd put my trainers earlier. If Jan hadn't been so pissed off with me, I'm sure she would have removed my shoes herself, after I slumped onto the bed. I tied my laces and stood slowly, not wanting the bed to creak. I could make the window in a couple of strides and was glad I didn't have to go through the bedroom door. The floorboards in front of it groaned every time a foot was placed anywhere near them. Nevertheless, I stepped gingerly, my heart beating twenty to the dozen. I reached the window, lifted the latch-arm, and pushed it wide. It made a slight whine as it attained its limit, but not enough to penetrate the hubbub downstairs. Climbing through and descending the ladder would be the worst part.

I stood for a minute or so, working out the best way to manoeuvre myself through the gap. Luckily, the windowsill was level with my groin, so it wouldn't be too much trouble to swing my leg out. I gripped the sill and frame, pivoted, and pushed my left leg out. I felt around for the ladder and managed to place my foot on the third rung down. I slowly moved my weight from my right foot to my left, waiting to see if the ladder stayed firm; it did. I lifted my right leg and squeezed it through the small gap between the window frame and my own body. I was sweating. Ordinarily, it would have been a doddle, but, when you're trying to do it without making a sound, it's extremely stressful, believe me.

I straightened up, both feet on the ladder, both hands on the windowsill. Slowly, I began to ease myself down. It was probably less than a minute before my right foot hit terra firma, but it seemed a lot longer. I was standing between the dining room and the kitchen. Joni was in her 'Big Yellow Taxi' and Drake was entertaining the two women with another of his anecdotes. Just the same, I ducked down and crept under the kitchen window. Once I'd reached the passageway, leading to the front of the house, I breathed a silent sigh of relief. Barring a sudden fire, causing the three of them to run out of the front door, I should be home and dry, I thought.

I almost ran down the path but held myself back. At the moment silence was more important than speed. I looked at my watch; it was just after nine and the light was fading. I'd told Efram and Peter that I'd be at the beach as near to nine as possible and to wait for me. Once again, I mentally patted myself on the back for a job well done. Considering what a quivering mess I'd been not too long ago, I'd put in a sterling performance, under the circumstances. I emerged onto East Street and quickened my pace. Time to meet my partners and begin the destruction of Simon Drake and his filthy whore.

SIXTEEN

I saw no sign of Efram and Peter, as I approached the beach and my stomach did a back flip. Surely, nothing could have happened their end; that would be unfair. I walked onto the sand, the sun seeming to sink into the sea, praying. I seemed to be doing a lot of that just lately.

"Pssst."

I turned in the direction of the sound and saw Pete's head pop out from a rocky outcrop. I strode over.

"You did pretty well, by the looks of it," said Efram, looking at his watch. "We were settled in for a lengthy wait."

I let out a heavy sigh. "I thought something had happened, when I didn't see you."

"Well we thought we'd stay away from prying eyes, as much as possible," he replied.

The dinghy was inflated and ready to go, the oars laying across the top.

"I guess this is it then, chaps." I waved to the shoreline. "Shall we?"

"I can't wait," said Peter. "Let's do it and do him as well."

Efram smiled. "He thinks he's in a Stephen King novel. I don't know if that's a good or bad thing."

"As far as I'm concerned, he can think what he likes as long as we manage to achieve our goal."

"We'll soon find out, I guess," said Efram grimly. "Give us a hand with this thing, will you. I don't want to drag it; in case it gets caught on a sharp rock. Another puncture at this time wouldn't be good."

I nodded and grabbed the back end while he lifted the front. My stomach had discarded the back flip for a continuous session of forward rolls. There were so many emotions fighting for supremacy, my head was reeling.

We made our way to the sea, Peter hobbling at our side. I noticed the leg brace had gone and all he had was a stick. Every time I saw him, his movement seemed to have improved.

"You soon won't need that thing," I told him, pointing to the stick.

He grinned. "Maybe that'll be sooner than you think. I've got a particularly good feeling about all of this."

I smiled back. "We've got to put our trust in the big feller, I guess. I have to admit, I've been talking to him a fair bit recently."

"And he's listening, believe me," he said with conviction.

"I hope you're right, Peter. I really do."

"Okay," said Efram. "Let's get this baby in the water." He paddled into the sea until he was up to his knees. I followed; a dinghy length behind. We lay the rubbery craft on the surface and climbed in, Peter first. Efram assumed the rower's position, oars in hand. I clambered in last, and we all sat there for a minute or two, making sure we could hear no air escaping.

"Right," said Efram. "Here we go."

He began to row and, after a few minutes, had mastered the action and no longer had us going around in circles.

"It's been a while," he said apologetically.

"Well I haven't rowed a boat since I was a kid," I admitted.

"Me neither," he said with a grin.

All that was left of the sun, by now, was a tiny golden triangle of ripples. The moon was resplendent in a cloudless, star crazed sky. The difference between here and London still amazed me. It was like going from the TV of the sixties to 4K. Every single star was crystal clear. The sea took on a silver sheen.

"That is beautiful," I sighed, looking up.

"Yes," Efram agreed. "It certainly is."

"That's a righteous sky," said Peter. "God is watching over us."

Efram looked at him and smiled. "I wish I had your faith, son."

"You will have, Dad. Wait and see."

The more I listened to Peter, the more convinced I became that we could pull this off. I still couldn't believe that I was considering the existence of a supreme being and that he may throw his weight behind our cause. As Efram had said, I wished I had the boy's faith.

It took us about ten minutes to reach the island and, by the time we pulled the dinghy onto the beach, Efram was bent over, breathing heavily.

"You should have let me do that," I said to him.

"I'm fine, "he gasped. "Just a bit out of practice, that's all."

I dragged the dinghy up, out of the water and Peter manoeuvred his way out. He stood and sniffed. "Do you smell that?" he asked.

I took in a deep breath, discerning nothing above the odour of ozone and seaweed. I shook my head. "What?"

He grinned again. "The sweet smell of success."

I looked him in the eye. "I smell something else."

He immediately lifted his arm and sniffed the pit. "I had a shower this afternoon," he said.

I squeezed his shoulder. "A breath of fresh air," I said. "You're a real credit to your mum and dad, and, I really mean that." I was starting to well up.

"And Charlie will be a credit to you and Jan," he said softly.

That was it. The tears that I'd managed to contain within my lower lids spilled over, and it took all my self-control to stop myself breaking down altogether. Peter put his hand on my arm and whispered in my ear.

"The vicar's history."

Efram had started to weave his way through the rocks. I hugged Peter. "If Charlie's a boy," I said to him. "I want him to be as optimistic and resourceful as you."

"Are you two coming?" Efram asked impatiently.

The torch he had with him wasn't needed. It seemed that even the moon was on our side. Although the light was a little eerie, reminiscent of the old horror films, it was bright enough to illuminate the rock's terrain. We followed a well-trodden path from the beach into the heart of the island. Clumps of broom grew wildly, their yellow blossom, accentuated in the moonlight.

"Do you have any idea where to look?" I asked Peter.

He thought for a moment. "Not exactly," he replied. "But I think I'll know when we're close."

"But you're not sure." I was desperate for assurance. I so wanted this journey to be the beginning of the end for Drake.

"He won't let us down," Peter said, smiling. "You need to believe that."

It's hard to put faith into a being that, until recently, was a fantasy figure, a reason for so many wars, and the mascot of a huge money-making machine.

I had never really thought much about the existence of God before coming to Chanter's Hide. It's so much easier to sit on the fence, let's face it. Now though, I really wanted him to be the omnipresent body that his followers believed him to be - the pure essence of good.

"I'm trying my best, Peter, I really am," I said to him. "It's just that, after all these years of thinking of him as some sort of mythical Gandalf, it's hard, you know?"

The moonlight shone on his teeth as he grinned. "Maybe he is like Gandalf," he said. "He was pretty awesome, after all."

Despite myself, I chuckled. "Yeah, I guess he was."

We continued inward and upward along the path, the occasional rabbit hopping in front of us, oblivious to any danger we may present. I looked back over to the beach at Chanter's Hide, making sure no-one from the village had decided on a moonlit boat trip. Myriad windows were illuminated, and the scene looked homely and peaceful, a perfect picture of coastal, village life. Without a Satanist in charge, I suppose it would be. I wondered if the rest of the Hiders really felt affection for their vicar, or if they were, like us, terrified of him. I tended to lean toward the latter. If that really was the case, we were doing this, as much for them, as ourselves.

Ahead, Efram stopped, hands on his knees. I hadn't realised how steep the path had been until we reached the top. I was much younger that Efram and a lot fitter. Peter was carried by his faith.

He was puffing and panting when I drew level with him and Peter.

"I am so out of shape," he managed between breaths. "When this is over, I'm going to start jogging."

"Maybe you ought to stop making huge pansful of mashed potato," said Peter, chuckling. "Oh," he added. "And eating most of them."

"Yeah," he gasped. "Salad from now on – and fruit," he said as an afterthought.

We appeared to be on a rim that ran around the top of the rock. Half a dozen paths led down inside. The foliage was dark and thick.

"At least it's downwards from now on," Efram said gratefully.

"Are you getting anything yet?" I asked Peter, hopefully.

He stuck out his bottom lip and shook his head. "Not yet."

"Which path do we take?" Efram asked him.

"I don't know." If a person can snarl in an apologetic manner – he did. "Does it matter? They all go downwards, don't they?"

I looked at Efram and he returned my gaze.

"And don't look at each other like that either," Peter said accusingly. "When I feel something, I'll let you know. Okay?"

"I'm sorry son," murmured Efram.

"Me too, Pete. It's just that we're kind of relying on you. I know that's not fair, but........."

"But what? And it's Peter, not PETE. Got it?"

"Yeah, sure – sorry." I caught Efram's eye and he shook his head in a 'leave it' sort of gesture.

"Maybe we should have a rest," he suggested.

"Why? Because I'm a cripple. Or because you're fat, old and totally out of shape?" Peter said harshly.

"Peter, what's wrong?" I asked softly.

At first, he glared at me. Then his expression softened.

"I'm sorry," he mumbled. "There is something so evil here." He looked into my eyes and I saw the fear.

"But we can beat it, can't we?" I held him by the shoulders. "Can't we?"

"I.....d...don't know," he said softly.

I shook him. "You said, he was history," I said with a snarl. "That's what you said."

Efram grabbed my arm and I was surprised at the strength in his grip. "For God's sake, Ben. Leave the boy alone."

I dropped my arms and felt my shoulders slump. "So, what happened to God kicking his arse? All of this – have faith shit. What happened to all that?" I was almost in tears.

"He probably will," Peter, almost, whispered.

It was my turn to glare at him. "Probably? Probably? What good is probably?"

Efram put his arm around my shoulders and squeezed tight. He put his mouth to my ear.

"Leave Peter alone," he said sharply. "And start behaving like a man."

I sucked in air, fighting back the tears. It was only then, I realised I'd been relying on a child to sort this shit out. I'd been hiding behind Peter's faith – relying on it. Putting my wife's and child's survival onto the shoulders of a young boy. A boy with polio, to boot, albeit in the latter stages.

I tried to smile, took his face in my hands. "It'll be fine, Peter." I winked at him.

"He's history."

"Let's get on with this before I have to bang your heads together," Efram growled. He put his arm around his son. "We are all in this together, it's not down to you to sort everything out. Remember that."

I realised I'd been dumping all my stress on Peter's shoulders and felt ashamed.

"I'm sorry Peter, I'll try and stop relying on you to bolster my own confidence. Like your Dad just said, it's time I started acting like a man."

I gave him an apologetic smile. "I promise to act more like a responsible adult, from now on," I said firmly.

"That would be appreciated," said Efram. "Now, which path are we going to take?"

I walked over to the third from the left. "As no-one has any preference, we'll take this one." It felt good to have made a decision.

Efram held out his arm in a 'after you' kind of gesture. I looked down, seeing the pale dusty path disappearing into thick gorse bushes, hugged by, what seemed to be, twisted ash and poplar trees. Under the pale light of a Dorset moon, it appeared to beckon and threaten at the same time.

"Are you going to get a move on?" Efram asked impatiently.

I nodded, swallowed hard and put my best foot forward. "I'm all over it," I whispered, fighting the urge to turn around and get the hell off this God forsaken rock. I began to move slowly downwards, my heart beating like a heavy metal band's bass drum. To begin with the going was easy, but, before too long, the bushes and trees closed in, the brambles tearing at our clothes and skin.

"I can't see Drake putting up with this," Efram said, unhooking himself from a particularly brambly briar.

"He probably casts some sort of spell and it all parts like the Red Sea did for Moses," I said as another thorn drew more blood from my calf. "How are you doing Peter?" I called back.

"Fine," he replied. I could tell his teeth were gritted. I felt humbled. This boy had so much mental strength, it was unbelievable.

We plodded on, deeper and deeper. The trees were now closing ranks above our heads and the moonlight was slowly being smothered.

"Have you got that torch?" I asked Efram.

He handed it to me, and I switched it on, in time for the beam to show the largest adder I'd ever seen slide across the path in front of me. I shuddered.

We pushed on, waiting for the foliage to reduce, as it had to – surely. I didn't know what we were looking for but there had to be some sort of communal area for Drake and his followers to do whatever it was they did.

"Little bugger," hissed Efram, slapping his neck. "It bit me."

Soon we were all waving our hands, slapping our heads and necks. I shone the torch and could see tiny, red spiders dropping from the trees. They were only small, but they were eating us alive. I started to run, ignoring the briars, panic setting in.

It was probably less than two minutes but, it seemed like an eternity, before we lurched out of the bushes and tumbled to the ground, the moon back in view.

All three of us were still slapping at any piece of exposed skin. I could even feel a couple of the little beggars biting my chest, under my T shirt. I did my Tarzan impression and ended their filthy lives.

"They might be small," I said. "But their bite bloody hurts." I looked at the tiny specks of blood that covered my hands and arms. I wiped my face with the palm of my hand. It came away smeared red.

"I hate spiders," hissed Efram, shuddering. "Especially ones with teeth."

"I think I chose the wrong path," I said apologetically.

Peter shook his head. "It wouldn't have mattered which one you'd chosen," he said flatly. "We're not welcome here."

"Do you mean they were some kind of defence mechanism?" I asked him.

"I think we may find that our village vicar has quite a few surprises up his sleeve," he replied. "I just hope they don't act like a two-way radio."

"Do you mean those disgusting little objects could be alerting him to our presence here?" Efram asked his son.

Peter shrugged. "It wouldn't surprise me."

"In that case," I said. "We'd better get a move on." I was tired of being weak and afraid. Sick of being a pathetic person who relied on a young boy to fight his battles for him. It was time to take control. "Are you feeling anything yet," I asked Peter. He shook his head.

"Right, let's see what else Drake has in store for us, and find the last piece of this bloody puzzle."

Efram looked at me, smiled and nodded slowly, his expression one that said – that's more like it.

We were on a kind of plateau, peppered with rocky outcrops and more broom. Wisps of cloud had begun to sully the night sky but, did little to dim the moon's sparkle. I began to walk to the far side of the clearing, scanning left and right as I went.

"Keep your eyes peeled for three headed dogs," I said.

"My God, a joke?" The surprise was evident in Efram's tone.

"Who's joking?" I said.

We crossed the plateau, however, without being attacked by any more of Drake's minions. It appeared to be a flat space with only one way in or out. That's unless, we fancied climbing down a, practically, sheer cliff-face.

"Spiders or no spiders, I definitely chose the wrong path," I said, unable to hide the deflation I was feeling.

"Maybe you were led to choose that path," said Peter excitedly. "Come and take a look at this."

We hurried over to where Peter was standing, apparently looking down over the side of the plateau.

"I think we may have hit pay dirt," said Efram.

I followed their gaze. Steps had been roughly hewn into the rock, going down into the heart of the island. I patted Peter on the back. "Well done, Peter. I think you may have come up trumps. Do you feel anything yet?"

He looked crestfallen and I felt terrible. After deciding to stand on my own two feet and take control of things, here I was again, putting pressure on the poor lad. I smiled at him. "I'm sorry, I promise I'll stop asking you that. Should I go first?"

Efram tipped me the wink. He seemed pleased with the new me.

"Lead on, young man," he said, punching me on the shoulder.

When I mentioned that the steps had been roughly hewn into the rock, I may have been a little more complimentary than I should have. They were extremely uneven and even treacherous in places.

"Be very careful, Peter," I called back. "This is a bit tricky."

"If I fall, you'd better catch me," he said jokingly.

"Roger that," I said, and I meant it. I could feel the blood coursing through my veins. I felt alive, the contempt I held for Drake being converted into positive energy.

"Bugger," I heard Efram exclaim. "He certainly doesn't make things easy, does he? I nearly went base over apex then."

"Take your time," I told him. "I don't fancy catching the pair of you, especially after all those mashed spuds."

"Very amusing," said Efram. "You look after yourself, don't worry about me, I'll be just fine."

I carried on down. At least there was no foliage above, filled with tiny, cannibalistic spiders. Small mercies, as they say. The staircase spiralled into the centre of the rock and soon the moon disappeared from view as we entered a steep tunnel. I switched the torch back on, taking a little more care with each step.

"I wonder how far it goes down," Efram called. His voice seemed to boom in the relatively confined space.

"Just so long as it doesn't go all the way to hell," Peter said.

"I take it, that was a joke?" I asked him.

"I think so," he said. There was, thankfully, humour in his tone.

"Buggeration," Efram spat. "This tunnel isn't made for the larger man. "I've just scraped my elbow, now."

"Man up, will you," I said.

"Yeah Dad, man up," Peter agreed.

The darkness was like a black wall, the torch's beam struggling against its suffocation. Claustrophobia's frantic fingers clawed at my throat and I forced myself to steady my breathing. I am in control, I am in control, I kept telling myself. I hoped the more I said it, the more believable it would become. I focused on Efram's puffing and blowing, punctuated with the occasional 'bugger' or 'blast'. By doing that, I managed to keep calm and keep shuffling one foot in front of the other.

"It's really dark," Peter said softly.

"You can say that again, son," Efram agreed. "That torch doesn't seem to be making a great deal of difference, either."

"Well it's all we've got, so cut the griping," I called over my shoulder.

I heard Efram chuckle. "You've certainly changed your tune," he said.

"I think you'll agree, I needed to," I said flatly.

"Oh, don't get me wrong, I'm not complaining. Old Ted would have been proud of you."

SEVENTEEN

I hadn't thought about the old chap for a while, apart from to curse him for leaving us his cottage, in the first place. Now though, I admired him for standing up to Drake, especially considering his age. Here was me, less than half his age, still fighting the urge to turn and flee. I vowed that I would avenge the poor old chap. I would make Drake pay for whatever it was he did to him.

"What was he really like?" I asked Efram. "I only met him briefly a couple of times."

"He was fearless" Efram replied. "Put me to shame. He was a proud man, with the heart of a lion."

"And you have no idea at all how he died?"

"Like I told you before, Drake took care of everything. Said to me – oh by the way, Ted died of a heart attack, last night."

"You never saw his body?"

Efram sighed. "No, I didn't. I went back into my cottage and closed the door. The look in Drake's eye was enough. I still regret not being able to say goodbye to him."

"I liked Ted," said Peter.

"Yes, I know you did; and he liked you too, son. Mind you, I would have preferred it if he had made sure you were out of earshot, when he effed and blinded."

"He used to make me laugh," Peter recalled.

I wondered if we were talking about the same man. My most enduring memory of Ted was how miserable and cantankerous he had been. Still, he had never had much to do with the family; Efram was, after all, his friend.

"It's beginning to level out," I said.

"Is there a light at the end of the tunnel?" Efram asked.

"Not yet, I'm afraid," I replied apologetically.

"We are really close," said Peter. The tone of his voice indicating the disgust he felt. "I can practically smell the stink."

I sniffed the air, but, obviously, didn't possess Peter's olfactory skills, when it came to rooting out evil. I was about to ask him if anything was occurring in the opposite direction but stopped myself. It was not helpful for any of us, for me to keep pestering the lad. Instead, I listened to Efram puffing and blowing and prepared myself, as best I could, for whatever lay ahead. I tried to recall some of the manuscripts I'd read in the past, centring on the black arts. Unfortunately, all I could remember was the constant bringing forth of the devil, in various guises. The most popular being a goat. I was beginning to regret not taking those subscriptions more seriously, even though the composition, in most cases, had been horrendous. Some had seemed like textbooks on the occult, even though they were submitted as fictional. Those were the ones I was trying to dredge up. The problem was – I'd only read the first few pages, made the decision, and rejected them. Unless I decreed that the author showed promise, my P.A. Jenny would have sent out the usual – thank you, but no thank you letter. Now, I was wishing I'd been less hasty. But hey, we all have regrets. Efram dragged me from my thoughts.

"Has anybody got any idea how much longer this damned tunnel is?" He hissed. "I'll have no skin left."

Even though I could see no light, other than that of the torch, Peter answered him. "Not too much further now, Dad."

Efram sighed. "Thank God for that,"

I was about to ask Peter how he knew, when the light at the end of the tunnel began to make an appearance.

"However long the tunnel," I said. "We will all, eventually, see the light."

"Very profound, I'm sure," said Efram. "Just get a move on, will you?"

I pushed on, the moonlight becoming more accessible again. My undiscerning sense of smell was, suddenly, on red alert. The stink that Peter had mentioned earlier was starting to penetrate my heathen nostrils. There was a burnt, coppery aroma that almost made me wretch.

As we emerged from the tunnel, Efram's sigh of relief was followed by a gagging cough. "That's awful," he spluttered.

The moonlight showed several irregular stone slabs, surrounding something that resembled an altar. There were various markings in the grass and soil, some painted, some sliced and dug out. Although I'd never smelled it before, I knew the reek that was suffocating me was that of blood and burnt flesh. I retched, Efram threw up, Peter stood with his lip curled in disgust.

Now there was no avoiding the question. I needed positivity.

"Peter," I said, a little more forcefully than intended. "Anything?"

There were tears in his eyes. "There is so much evil in this place," he said in a whimper. "So many have suffered here."

I didn't possess Peter's gift, but even I could feel the corruption, emanating from the very soil beneath our feet. This was little more than a slaughterhouse. I looked at the altar and imagined young babies lying there crying in terror, just before their short lives were ended. I didn't try to stop the tears; they were all I had to give.

"Good God in Heaven," whispered Efram, wiping his mouth with the back of his hand. "This is a terrible place."

I regained a little of my composure and asked the question again.

"Are you feeling anything that might help us, Peter."

He shook his head. "It's smothering everything," he moaned. "It's everywhere."

I knew what he meant. The stench seemed to seep into my pores, claw at my throat. This was only a couple of steps up from hell itself.

Efram retched again. He held up his hand. "I'm sorry," he spluttered. "That awful stink just gets down you."

"We have to do something," I said, my cheeks wet with sorrow. "We have to find what we came for. We have to stop this."

Peter cleared his throat and straightened his back. "You're right, Ben," he agreed, a steely determination in his young voice. "Standing here feeling sorry for ourselves isn't going to get us anywhere. This foul business has to be ended, once and for all."

Efram looked at his son, his pride shining like a beacon. "Where do we start?"

"I guess we do the same as we did before Peter found the tunnel down to this abattoir," I suggested.

Peter nodded. "Spread out. I don't know what we're looking for but, I'm sure we will, when we find it."

I was devastated that we were no further forward than that, but it was what it was. I don't think any of us were too keen on splitting up, but when the devil drives, and all that. An unfortunate turn of phrase, under the circumstances. I glanced at Efram. He was still looking a little green around the gills.

"You okay?" I asked him.

"Not really," he replied. "You?"

"I've been better," I said, trying to muster a grin but failing miserably.

"What is he?"

It was obvious who he was talking about. "I don't know. All I do know is that before coming to this village, the devil was a myth and the jury was still out regarding the man upstairs."

He nodded. "Well, we'd better get on with it, I suppose."

Reluctantly, we gave each other the thumbs up and parted company.

As we walked amongst the stained, stone slabs, pictures sprang into my mind. Drake conducting his disciples in an orgy of disgusting degradation, whipping them into a frenzy before the main event. I stopped the film show there and then. I could not envisage what would happen to Jan and Charlie if we failed.

In fact, failure was not an option. My wife and child were depending on me, even if, at the moment, they didn't know it. Ignorance, in Jan's case, was definitely bliss. I despised the vicar more than I had ever hated anyone or anything else before but, for the time being, I was happy for Jan to think he was one step down from the Almighty.

"Oh God, this is disgusting," Efram groaned. "I don't know what I'm stepping in, half of the time."

I nodded grimly. The ground was splattered with excrement and bodily fluids. More images tried to leap into my mind, but I forced them back. I had to stay focused and not let Drake or any of his abhorrent practices get into my head. I gagged a couple of times but managed to keep the contents of my stomach intact. The same, however, couldn't be said for poor, old Efram. He was retching every couple of minutes.

"What was that?" I heard him say. I looked over to where he was standing, about twenty yards away. He was peering into the gloom. As I was trying to see what was concerning him, I heard a rustling sound behind me. I turned around quickly, my heart rate quickening. A bank of cloud had decided to creep across the moon. I flicked on the torch and gasped.

A line of spiders, the size of rats was creeping towards us, their eyes white and lifeless. Strings of repulsive drool hung from their gaping maws. I shone the torch, in an arc, over to where Efram was standing. He leapt back when the beam revealed the reason for his disquiet.

"Jesus," he exclaimed. "They're huge. I hate spiders."

Peter was at the apex of our little triangle and still searching. He heard his father and turned.

"What's wrong?" He asked.

"We're not on our own," I said, shuffling backwards, shining the torch back and forth. Efram began to move back too, muttering 'oh my God, oh my God' over and over to himself. I have to say that spiders had never bothered me before I came to this damned rock; in fact, if ever I'd found one in the house, I'd always used the 'glass and card' business to release it into the wild. These monstrosities, however, were a different kettle of fish. As we moved back, they kept pace with us. There were hundreds of them. I wondered why they didn't scurry all over us; we'd be helpless if they did.

"Keep moving this way," said Peter. "Are you okay, Dad?"

"Not really, son," he replied quietly.

"Don't make any sudden movements," Peter said. "Slowly does it. I may have found a way out."

If those last words were music to my ears, they must have been a full-blown symphony to Efram's.

We both backed slowly to where Peter was standing, neither of us taking our eyes off our arachnid friends. Efram shivered.

"Filthy little beggars," he said. I think the similarity to Humphrey Bogart in 'The African Queen' was accidental. He was, certainly, in no mood for impressions.

"What have you found?" I asked Peter, not turning my head.

"It's another tunnel," he replied.

"This rock is a bloody maze," I said. I suddenly had a flashback to our dinner date at Drake's house. "Which way does it go?"

"I'm not sure," Peter said slowly. "But I think it'd heading back towards where we moored the dinghy."

"Or, maybe back to the village?"

"What do you mean – back to the village?" Efram chimed in.

"You're supposed to be on your father's side," Efram said, grinning.

"There are only two sides," I pointed out. "Us and them. The good and the bad."

"Who's the ugly?" Efram asked.

We both looked at him and smiled. He shook his head.

"Let's get on with it."

"And remember," I said. "To quote Mr. Dylan – God's on our side."

EIGHTEEN

"As I recollect, as Peter mentioned earlier, he was also on Hitler's," said Efram.

"Dad," Peter said. "Will you start being more positive?" He sighed. "How many more times?"

"I was just saying." He jerked a thumb at me. "He started down the Bob Dylan route, not me."

"Was I really this bad?" I asked the two of them.

"Yes," they said in unison.

"Well, enough – from all of us. Let's just do what we have to do. No more negativity. Agreed?"

"I'm with the programme," said Peter.

"What about you, Porthos – are you with the programme?" I asked Efram.

"Stop being so stupid and shine that torch back down this tunnel, will you?"

I smiled and did as I was told. For a while we trudged on in silence. I started to think about Jan and Hannah and when Drake would decide to make his move. The thought terrified me. Unfortunately, more thoughts raced into my mind and I had to usher them out and close the door. This was not the time to be thinking about what would happen if we didn't stop the bastard. We had to stop him.

The torch had become dimmer over the past five minutes or so and I prayed it would get us to our destination, without failing completely. If not, we were in the dark; there would be nothing we could do about it.

"I don't suppose you've got any spare batteries, have you?" Efram whispered in my ear. I hadn't noticed him sidling up beside me and he made me jump.

"They're rechargeable," I said with a wink. "We'll be able to recharge them when we get to the rectory. I'm sure Simon won't mind."

I could hear Peter sniggering, but Efram wasn't amused.

"It was a simple question. We'll be floundering about in the dark soon."

"If my calculations are correct," I said. "We should reach base with twenty seconds to spare."

Efram made a 'harrumph' sound. "Sarcasm is the lowest form of wit," he said.

"We can't be that far away now – really," I said.

"No, we're nearly there," said Peter excitedly.

The scene revealed by the diminishing beam gave nothing away.

"You can feel something?" I asked.

"It's definitely up ahead," he said slowly. Although I couldn't see his face, by his tone, I imagined his brow to be furrowed.

"What else?"

"I think it's very well protected," he said. "Sorry."

I reached out and patted him on the back. "All that matters is that we're on the right track, and you, have nothing to be sorry for. You're a role model to both of us." I nudged Efram.

"I'm enormously proud of you, son. Enormously proud, indeed."

The drips from the roof of the tunnel had ceased and the temperature had taken an upward turn. I took this to mean we were walking beneath the earth instead of the sea. The air seemed thicker and I knew we weren't far away from Drake's lair.

"I think this definitely leads to the rectory," I said, more to myself than either of the others.

"We're almost there," Peter confirmed.

"I don't suppose either of you has a plan?" Efram asked.

"We just play it by ear," I said with a shrug. "We don't know where we're going to enter Chanter House, or what we're going to find when we do. We can't plan for the unknown."

"We need to get in there, find the last piece of our jigsaw and get out," said Peter.

I shone the torch towards Efram. I could see he was about to say something that would be neither helpful, nor positive. I drew my finger and thumb across my lips and gave him a meaningful stare. He closed his mouth and nodded slowly.

When I shone the torch back to the tunnel, it appeared to be better maintained than the leaky stretch we'd already travelled. I wondered if Drake used it much. I had decided, there was no doubt, he must know about it.

The cavern had been, more or less, straight from the island. Now it took a sharp turn and inclined upward.

"I think we're on the home stretch," I said quietly. I looked at Peter. He nodded. I could see the fear in his eyes and thought, it was probably reflected in my own. I patted him on the shoulder and tried to smile. I couldn't recall a time in my entire life when I had felt less like smiling. Nevertheless, I managed a fair impression.

"Is that a door?" Efram asked suddenly.

I peered up ahead and, sure enough, a large, oak door stretched across the tunnel.

We all started to walk slowly, listening hard. Caution was the name of the game, from now on. We reached the door and I put my ear to the wood. At that moment, I'm sure we were all holding our breath. I could hear nothing.

"It probably leads into the cellar," I whispered.

"That would make sense," Efram agreed.

There was a round, rusted, iron handle with a keyhole below it. My heart sank. What if it was locked? As if reading my mind Peter said softly.

"It won't be locked, will it? I mean, why would he lock it? That would be ridiculous."

"There's only one way to find out," I said.

I turned the handle and the door swung inwards easily and noiselessly.

Instinctively, we all took a step back, our communal sharp intake of breath, held. Peter's warning about 'it' being well protected was foremost in my mind.

There was no light. I stood for a few minutes - or it seemed that long – listening. My thumb hovered over the nub that activated the torch. My fight or flight response was veering towards flight again, I'm afraid. I closed my eyes for a moment or two, steadied my breathing and pressed the button.

"That's a lot of wine," Efram whispered.

He wasn't wrong. The cellar – or should I say, wine cellar – was well stocked indeed. Many of the bottles were covered in cobwebs, and I felt Efram cringe, as a spider, resembling a normal house variety, dropped from one of the racks and scuttled across the floor.

"I can't help it," he said apologetically. "My mother was terrified of the little buggers. I guess she passed it on." He shook his head. "I mean, why does anything need that many legs?"

I swung the fading beam across the cellar, having to move forward to follow the dwindling light. It seemed, apart from a few manageable arachnids and numerous bottles of Chanter's Hide's best wine, we were alone.

"I don't suppose it's in here?" I asked Peter.

"Afraid not," he said.

"I think there's a flight of stairs over there," said Efram.

I shone the torch over again. "Try to curb your enthusiasm," I said, feeling as much trepidation as he did. "On......"

"Do not say it," Efram said.

"I think you should go first, Ben," Peter said.

His confidence in me was heart-warming. How I wished I had similar faith.

"Well, if nobody's fighting me for it – here goes."

Luckily, due to the age of the building, the steps were stone. I began the ascent gingerly, my heart thumping like it was going out of date.

At the top of the stairs, another door barred the way. I stopped and breathed a sigh of relief.

Peter was already at my back. "Is it locked?"

I had to muster every ounce of courage I possessed to put my hand on the handle. Before turning it, I put my ear to the wood – nothing.

"Do you think they're waiting for us?" I asked.

"If they are, we aren't inundated with options," Peter pointed out.

"Can you hear anything?" Efram asked.

I told him I couldn't.

"I think you'd better open the door then," he said, "standing here in the dark isn't going to get us very far, is it?"

"At least we're still alive," I said.

"Are you telling me – you want to run away?"

I turned the handle.

I've heard the phrase – time seemed to stand still – so many times, and thought, you know – cut the drama. Time never stands still; its passage is unerring. It appears to pass more quickly when enjoyment is involved and drags when boredom throws over its tedious blanket. That, however, is down to the amount of times the clock is perused. If I'm having a rare, old time, I seldom check my watch; if I'm bored out of my skull, I'm there every three or four minutes. Maybe I'm beginning to disprove my original theory. If time can appear to go quicker or slower, why can it not seem to stop. I was mentally rambling, not wanting to push that door.

"Is it locked?" Efram asked. I think I detected hope in his tone.

I pushed gently and it opened, again without a sound. I slowly put my head around the edge. On my left was the front door. Memories came flooding back. Although I was putting on a brave face on my second visit to Chanter House, inside, I was more terrified than the first time. I looked down the hall and listened carefully. I could hear muffled voices, but they came from the rear of the house – probably the kitchen. Even so, my heart sank. I suppose I'd always hoped that the place would be empty. I turned back to Efram.

"They're here," I whispered, "In the kitchen, I think."

Efram ushered me on. I don't know if he was eager to get to it, or just keen to get away from the spiders in the cellar.

"Be careful, Ben," Peter said, behind him. I held up a thumb/index finger circle and stepped into the hall. Within seconds the three of us were standing in Drake's hallway. I pushed the cellar door shut, and we stood, for a few moments, listening. I could make out Drake's and Shona's voices and assumed they were alone. Then my heart turned to ice. I heard Jan's voice. It sounded all dreamy – like she'd been drugged.

"He's got Jan," I said, and lurched forward. Efram grabbed my arm.

"Don't," he whispered in my ear. "You'll be playing into his hands."

"They're safe, until he takes them to the island," Peter said quietly. "We have to do what we came to do, otherwise we'll be no help to Jan anyway. Please Ben: I know it's hard, but we have no choice."

I was shaking as I looked them both in the eye, knowing they were right but still wanting to charge in and rip the bastard limb from limb. Only I knew, it wouldn't go that way. If that were possible, I'd have done it days ago.

"Who's that?" Efram asked.

Another voice, weak with either fear or narcotics said, 'We're ready, Simon."

"That's Hannah," I said flatly. "She's due about the same time as Jan." I felt as if my whole world had come crashing down. "He's one step ahead, all the time."

"Maybe he thinks he is," Peter said. "We can't give up now. Come on Ben, you've got to fight for your wife and child. We just have to focus. Okay?"

NINETEEN

The term – emotional turmoil – is widely used. Mostly, by people who have never experienced it, and probably never will. I looked at Peter, knowing he was right, my chest, a huge box of fervent fireworks. When your wife and unborn child are behind a door, metres away, in the company of a Satanist, it's difficult to focus on anything else. Nevertheless, I pointed to the dining room door and began to creep towards it. The kitchen was behind the dining room, so we would be able to listen to what was being said, without being in full view should either Drake or his whore decide to leave the kitchen.

Silver-grey patches stretched across the floor and I was glad it was a clear night. We stood just inside the door of the dining room and listened. For once, I was glad the vicar liked the sound of his own voice. The walls in the rectory were substantial, to say the least, and had Drake been softly spoken, we would have had difficulty making out his words. As it was, he might as well have had a megaphone.

"Nearly time ladies," he said. "Soon you and your little ones will aid me in opening the great doorway."

"What time is Porter coming for us?" It was Shona's voice.

"He's got to make a few trips to get everyone over there first. Then he'll come up here for the guests of honour."

"We could always go through the tunnel."

"And deny our friends the great entrance. No, we do this with all the pizzazz, it deserves. This is what we've worked for. Tonight, our lord will take his rightful place." Drake laughed. "I know you're eager, my sweet but try and exercise a little more patience. We've waited so long for this; another hour isn't going to make much difference."

My fingernails were digging into the palms of my hands and I could feel the blood starting to trickle from the cuts. I put my arms around the other two.

"Does he mean who I think he means?" I whispered.

Peter nodded.

"The devil?"

He nodded again.

"We have to find the last piece, and quickly," I said. "We have to be back on that island when he makes his grand entrance. Peter?"

"I don't think it's down here," he said.

"Well, you'd better follow me then." I said, heading towards the staircase. "And watch out for snakes."

"Not again." Efram's fear was almost tangible.

"And I'm afraid it's just down to us this time," I said, not wanting to remind him of the part his wife's ashes had played but needing him to be fully focused. I was expecting him to emulate Indiana Jones but the only sound he made was a choked sort of groan.

Peter moved past me and limped up the stairs with a strange sort of grace. "I think I'd better go first. He reached the landing and moved along it like a sniffer dog, intent on pleasing his master. I followed him feeling inadequate. If this was a film, Efram and I were supporting actors, Peter, the leading man.

"Oh my God, we're close," he said softly.

I was about to congratulate him when I heard the chime of the doorbell. Drake hurried down the hall.

"Showtime folks," he said cheerily.

We froze.

He opened the front door. "'Evening George, everybody over there?"

"There and waiting," George replied.

"Good. Shona, are you ready?"

"I was born ready," she said seductively, slipping her arm through his.

"You're gorgeous," Drake said. "Isn't she, George?"

"Yes, gorgeous," he agreed.

Drake laughed. "Is that a gun in your pocket, George?"

"I.....I'm sorry," George spluttered.

"Don't worry, old chap. Tonight, all of the women will be exquisite and all of the men, rampant. Tonight, George, history will be made. Our Lord, imprisoned for so long, will finally be free. We will all be rewarded and know true satisfaction. Now, come on, the Great One has waited long enough." He paused, then. "Ah, ladies, are you ready to take your rightful places?"

I heard Jan and Hannah mumble something that sounded like reluctant assent.

"In that case – George, lead the way."

We waited until we heard the door shut.

"Jesus Christ, he's taken them," I said hoarsely, the panic, a slab of concrete in my chest. "We don't have a lot of time."

"I think he must have set his burglar alarm," Efram said shakily.

From one of the bedrooms, a cobra, the size of a python, slid out to face us, its hood extended. Its head moved back and forth, ready to strike.

"Don't move, Peter," I said.

"Why not?" There was no fear in his voice. He put his hand into his trouser pocket, pulled out the ankh and held it in front of the snake. It emitted a low hum. The tarnished, coppery appearance flashed briefly before becoming a solid, burnished gold. The cobra drew back its head, fangs exposed, hissing.

Peter pushed the ankh into its face. "Our fight is not with you, little one," he said. "Unless you make it so."

The snake turned and slithered away.

Efram let out the breath he had been holding. "That was awesome, son."

Peter put his hands over his eyes, his breathing steady. Efram and I waited, until he said. "It's in there." He pointed to, what appeared to be a closet.

"It looks like a cupboard," said Efram, echoing my thoughts. "There can't be much in there, surely."

"It's not a cupboard," Peter said.

I was about to ask how he knew, then decided not to waste any more time. At this moment Drake was taking my wife down to the beach, where a boat was waiting to take her to Smugglers' Rock, and her death. Time was something we didn't have a great deal of. I reached to open the door.

Peter laid his hand on my arm. "I'll do it, Ben."

I didn't argue. I stepped to one side.

"Be careful, son," Efram said.

Peter grasped the handle and pulled open the door. I don't know what I was expecting, but the space beyond the door wasn't it.

Efram gasped. "What the hell?"

The room was long and narrow. The only illumination was at the far end, where a dim, orange bulb hung above something that glittered. From this distance, it was impossible to tell what it was. Had that been the extent of it, all would have been hunky-dory. It wasn't.

The floor was a carpet of spiders. It was as if the entire arachnid population of Dorset was here. There were reddish, brown monstrosities with bodies the size of a heavyweight's fist, right down to the kind found lurking in the bathtub. They skittered over our feet. Efram nearly had a heart attack.

"Oh my God," he said, trying not to squeal like a girl. "There are millions of the dirty little buggers. Look at the size of that one!"

I didn't need to follow his gaze, the thing he was pointing to couldn't be missed. It had slithered to the floor from a hole in the wall, its body pulsating. It was as big as a football and it was looking at us. On its arrival, the rest of the spiders ceased there scurrying as if waiting for instructions.

"I think he may be the big cheese," I said, trying to make light of a situation that couldn't have been much heavier. "Am I right in thinking that we have to get through this lot and reach that thing under the bulb?" I asked Peter.

He shook his head. "No, I have to do that. You two need to wait here."

Even though Efram was terrified, he said. "We can't let you go in there on your own, son."

"You have no choice Dad. If you go in there, they'll be all over you in seconds and I won't be able to protect you. Some are venomous, the rest – well they'll crawl up your nose and into your mouth and block your airways. You'll be dead in minutes. I can't let that happen. You have to trust me." He looked into Efram's eyes. "Do you trust me, Dad?"

Efram swallowed, his expression a mixture of terror and pride. "I trust you, Peter. Please be careful. If I lost you, my life wouldn't be worth living anyway."

Peter hugged his father. "Have faith, Dad, have faith. Without it, we're all lost."

I know that Peter was Efram's son but, I'm sure I was just as concerned. Peter took a deep breath and stepped into the narrow room. He held the ankh out before him, its glow flickering slightly. He's just told his Dad to have faith, I thought, but it seems as if his own might be wavering a little. The smaller of the spiders scurried away from him and I saw the glow become steadier. I wanted to shout out, to urge him on, but I didn't want to break his concentration. I put my arm around Efram's shoulders. We were both holding our breath. I let mine out.

"You have a very special son," I said to him.

"Do you think I don't know that? All I've ever wanted was to keep him safe and now, it's the other way round. I should be doing that – not him."

"I think he's been chosen by someone of a higher rank," I said, pointing upward. "Just do as he says – have faith."

"That is easier said than done."

Peter was moving forward slowly and, although some of the spiders crept up over his shoes onto his legs, they fell back quickly and scuttled away. He was getting ever nearer to the bloated thing. It moved up and down slowly as if the long, hairy legs were spring loaded. It showed no sign of fear. I felt Efram shiver. "Please God, protect my son," he said softly.

Peter was about three metres away from the monstrosity now and I could see him falter. If he loses it now, I thought, we're all dead. I thought of Jan and Hannah being rowed over to that God forsaken rock. I forced myself to see what would happen to them and their unborn babies. I envisaged Drake standing over their pale, naked bodies with some sacramental dagger raised above his head, chanting as his followers indulged in all forms of debauchery. The picture was in my mind, in high definition and full colour. I saw Drake laughing as Shona pranced around him, her breasts swinging, caressing herself. I looked back to Peter. He was frozen to the spot. The huge spider was slithering towards him. It appeared to be grinning. "Jesus Christ, we're lost," I said, tears rolling down my cheeks. "Peter, "I shouted. "Keep the faith."

He turned and looked back. His face was a mask of terror.

"I...I... can't," he said.

In my mind's eye, I saw Drake howling with glee, triumphant, as he brought the dagger down. I charged across the room, waving my arms above my head.

TWENTY

"Please God, help us," I yelled, trampling myriad bodies underfoot. I reached Peter, yanked the ankh from his hand and landed with a thud in front of the grinning arachnid. I shoved it into those glaring, red eyes, never letting the picture of Jan leave my mind. It glowed like a piece of molten metal, taken from a blacksmith's fire. The spider let out a high-pitched wail and withered before me. I was on a roll. I pushed on.

"Watch out, Ben," I heard Efram shout.

I turned in time to see the biggest snake I'd ever set eyes on. It's hooded head, swaying from left to right, ready to strike.

The forked tongue of the king cobra flicked in and out. Its eyes were fixed on mine and I wondered if Drake could see through those black orbs. I was temporarily mesmerised. By the number of coils and the fact that we were face to face, I estimated its length to be in the region of fifteen metres.

"Ben!" I heard Peter say shakily. "Do something."

I held the ankh out before me, knowing deep down it wouldn't be enough. I refocused my mind on the horror Jan was about to face. I needed to see what I would be putting her through if I failed. The picture was back in my mind, and I held it there. I looked past the snake to the plinth beyond. A gold chain rested on a black, silk cloth - the third part of our puzzle. 'Hey big man, I could do with a bit of a hand here,' I said, returning my eyes to the cobra. I couldn't understand why it hadn't attacked. I looked deep into those snake eyes and said.

"God is on my side, you son of a bitch. Come on, show me what you've got. Are you frightened, because if you're not, you should be?"

The head swayed to and fro. I may have detected a little hesitation, but it was probably wishful thinking. I brought the image of Jan to the forefront of my mind until it appeared to merge with the black and yellow of the cobra.

"Ben. It's going to attack," Efram called from the doorway.

I saw the slight movement as the head went back.

"For Christ's sake, "I said. "We're on the same side. Please – help – me."

Everything happened in a flash, although I saw it all as if in slow motion. The snake's head reared and as it darted forward, the gold chain flew through the fetid air, spinning like a chainsaw's blade. Just before the fangs could penetrate my throat, the chain sliced the head from the cobra and wrapped itself gently around my neck. The ankh leapt from my hand and joined the chain. At that moment, I knew God existed. Within seconds, the spiders and snakes that had occupied the narrow room had scurried and darted into holes in the walls and we were alone.

The ankh throbbed against my chest, the chain warm and comforting around my neck. The fear I'd felt for Drake had disappeared. I was now a servant of the big man. For the first time in my life, I knew there was a God and that when he was really needed, he would be there for us.

"That was magnificent," said Peter. "I'm sorry I let you down, Ben."

I put a hand on his shoulder. "You didn't let anyone down, Peter. In fact, you showed me the way. This was always supposed to be down to me – not you. I am so grateful for all you've done."

"I don't know what to say," Efram said. "I take it all back. You kicked that thing's ass."

"I was only the tool," I said to him. "The big chap did all the heavy lifting. Now let's go and destroy the rest of the evil in this place. God really is on our side now."

"You betcha," said Peter.

"Lead the way," Efram said.

Within seconds we were in the cellar opening the door to the passage to Smugglers' Rock.

"Wait, I'll be a minute, "I said.

I darted back up the cellar steps, dashed into the kitchen and picked up the box of supersize matches laying by the gas hob. Seconds later I was in the dining room, splashing Drake's expensive cognac over the furniture and curtains. I lit two of the matches and threw one at the bottom of the curtains and the other on the brandy-soaked tablecloth. I picked up a bottle of malt whiskey and hurried back to the cellar. I splashed the liquor around the room and lit another three matches.

"Okay, lets' go," I said.

"You obviously intend to send everything back to hell," said Efram, with a satisfied smile.

I nodded. "If a job's worth doing."

Peter looked at me and I could see disappointment mixed with relief in his eyes.

"I still feel guilty - and stupid - for caving in, back there, "he said.

"I put my arm around him. "You did much more than should have been expected of you, Peter. This is my fight and always has been. I think that, maybe Ted chose me for this, to finish what he, so courageously, started. Now, with God's help, we'll witness the end of Drake's hold over this beautiful village."

"Hear, hear to that," said Efram.

"He knows we're coming," I said. "I can feel it. He won't make it easy for us, so be prepared."

"What, you mean more spiders and snakes?" Efram said, with a shudder.

"At least. Now let's go."

We plunged down the passageway, the smoke had already started to seep from Chanter House. I had never felt so alive. It was as if God himself were running along by my side. I glanced at Peter. It was incredible. He had discarded the walking stick and was keeping pace with only a trace of a limp. The difference between when I'd spotted him, on the beach, from up on the hill, hobbling along on sticks, his leg in a calliper to now, almost one hundred per cent fit was amazing.

"Oh, I do not believe this," I heard Efram say, his disgust evident.

Up ahead the tunnel floor was covered with every insect imaginable, and the stench was appalling. Cockroaches crawled over huge beetles, flies, the size of queen bees hovered in the air, whilst Efram's favourite – the spider was extremely well represented.

"Stand behind me," I said, "and hold onto my waist. Time to do the hokey cokey. All together – put your left leg in."

Peter grabbed hold of my waist and Efram brought up the rear. I grasped the ankh, feeling the chain tighten slightly around the back of my neck and stomped into the pile of this disgusting carpet. Every step I took was like Moses parting the Red Sea. Insects were suspended in mid-air, their legs trying to gain purchase on thin air.

"A walk in the park," Peter whispered in my ear.

"Don't count your chickens," I said to him. "This is just a little too easy. I'm thinking that Drake is still making his way to that filthy pit he uses as his 'temple'. Once he's there, with Jan and Hannah, he'll be able to focus. This is just the prelude."

"You don't know that."

I turned and looked him in the eye. "You know when you were getting your feelings, before, about the chain and the rest of it?"

He nodded.

"Well, these are no longer feelings. I know what we're going to be up against. And, believe me, it won't be a walk in the park. Drake isn't a spider you can crush under your boot."

"I'm guessing if God exists, the devil does too?" Efram said. By his expression, I knew he was hoping I was going to tell him not to be so stupid. Unfortunately, I couldn't do that.

"Drake's drawing his power from somewhere, "I said. "Obviously, not from God, so, what do you think?"

"It's the age-old fight between good and evil," Peter said enthusiastically.

"Yeah, but good doesn't always win," said Efram. "Have you taken a look at what's going on in this world of ours, lately?"

"Dad – will you stop being so negative." It was an order, rather than a question.

"He's right, Peter. We can't go into this thinking God's on our side and that's an end to it. If we don't play our parts with conviction and true belief, we're lost. Drake is on the verge of bringing Lucifer back from the abyss. He has worked years for this moment. He's not about to roll over and submit."

"Plus, he's an old hand at all of this," said Efram. "Don't forget that."

Although, I wanted us all to be prepared, Efram's continual 'bigging up' of the opposition was becoming a little tiresome and unhelpful.

"Which will give us an advantage," I said. "He sees me as a weak and irritating fly in his glorious ointment. He does not consider me a threat."

Peter nodded. "Never underestimate your opponent," he said.

"Exactly."

Efram didn't look convinced. "If you say so."

"I think his focus might have improved, "I said.

The insects were scurrying away. Our old pals, the snakes were back, and they'd brought their mates, the lizards along. They looked like kimono dragons on steroids.

"Jesus – is that an alligator?" Efram almost screamed.

It must have been about eight metres in length. It nudged the dragons aside with its long snout.

"You were saying, Peter?" I said, making eye contact with the beast. There was no fear in those dead eyes.

No-one moved. Drake's beast and I stared into each other's eyes, searching for weakness. I was no longer afraid.

"That thing is huge," Efram said.

"Be still," I said. "Both of you."

"Show yourself," I said to the alligator.

Those emotionless orbs stared back. The tail flicked suddenly to the side.

"Jesus." I felt Efram jump behind me.

I moved a step closer. "Show me," I said firmly.

The tail swished back the other way.

"I don't have time for this, Drake." I closed my eyes and breathed in, letting God take me. I looked down and saw Efram and Peter shaking with fear, the alligator's jaws opening and snapping back together. "I'm coming for you, "I said, only no words came from my mouth.

Drake left his servant and rose to meet me.

"You cannot win, the dark lord is almost amongst us."

"If you're so confident, why are you here, wasting time that could be spent finalising your lord's return?"

He smiled. "I am enjoying the game, Ben. I have to say I'm impressed with your bravado. I didn't think you had any fight in you."

I smiled back. "There is one difference between us. My Lord is with me already, whilst yours waits for a release that will never come. Your reign is about to come to an end."

The flicker was faint and fleeting, but it was there. Drake's conviction suffered a momentary lapse.

"Much as I'd like to continue this ludicrous conversation, my lord calls. Your wife and child are waiting to sacrifice themselves for his resurrection. It's a shame you'll miss the show. My friend below will be more than a match for you, I'm sure."

I watched his essence slide back to the floor of the cavern and disappear. It was time. Efram was shouting behind me. "Stay back, stay back."

"I thought I told you to be still," I said.

"You were just standing there. It moved forward."

"And now it will go back to where it came from," I said. I strode forward, both hands clasping the ankh, drawing the power that was all around me.

"Do you wish to confront the true Lord, "I asked the dead eyes. "Because he wishes to confront you."

I took my hands from the ankh, they were golden. I reached down and watched as the alligator's jaws snapped ineffectively. I placed my hands over the eyes and let the power flow. In my mind, I heard the screaming as Drake's manifestation twisted and flapped like fly caught in a spider's web.

"We're coming," I said. "Any evil that wishes to stand before us, take heed. God is in this place."

All the vicar's creations shrivelled and fell beneath our feet, as we made our way towards Smugglers' Rock.

"I never really believed in God," Efram said apologetically.

"Nor did I," I said.

"I never doubted his existence," said Peter. "We are about to save Jan and Hannah and set Chanter's Hide free, with God's help." He waved a hand around the carnage. "It is now obvious that Simon Drake and his miserable devil are no match for God's almighty power."

"Whoa, don't get ahead of yourself, Peter. This was only easy because Drake's attentions were occupied elsewhere. He is hours – no – minutes away from achieving his goal. The longer this goes on, the more powerful he becomes, and the closer the dark lord's resurrection. We may have won this paltry battle but, the war is still to come. When we get to the island……..."

"All hell breaks loose," said Efram.

"I couldn't have put it better myself."

"But we will win, won't we?" Peter looked deflated.

I put my arm around his shoulders. "With God's help and our bravery – yes, I believe we will. But I only know one thing for sure – if Drake harms my wife and our baby – I will kill him, with or without God's help. That's a promise."

"Don't forget," Peter said. "We are the three musketeers"

Efram grimaced. "Oh please, son, don't start that again."

"Let's just keep our wits about us," I said, "we're not too far away now, and remember, we're in this together. We all have our parts to play."

"I think it's getting a bit lighter," Efram said, without any enthusiasm.

He was right. We were nearing the end of the tunnel and the moonlight was beginning to cast vague shadows. I could hear the chanting. The Hiders were out in force, obeying their master's orders. I wondered if there was any way back for them, assuming we were successful. If we managed to keep Lucifer where he belonged and destroyed Drake, what would happen? Would they turn on us or would the spell be broken? Would the village become the idyllic hideaway that Jan and I had first thought it to be? These were questions that only time could answer. Since meeting the vicar and finding out his true intentions, my only desire was to get out of Dorset all together. I couldn't override those thoughts at that moment. Until this was over, one way or the other, it was pointless giving the matter any head space. I had to stay focused on the job in hand.

"Here we are, folks," I said, as the path started to rise. "It'll soon be show time."

Efram took in a deep breath and let it out nervously. "Let's do it," he said, unable to hide the tremor in his delivery.

"One for all and………."

"Please, Peter – stop. We are not in some Alexander Dumas novel, this is real life, and I, for one, am terrified."

TWENTY-ONE

The closer we came to our goal, the more I prayed we wouldn't be too late to save Jan and Hannah. I knew that I would only be able to achieve their release if we all stayed focused and believed. For a man who had never really considered God's existence before, leaning towards the atheist point of view in fact, it seemed ironic that I should be in this position. If my wife and child weren't about to be slaughtered in the name of the Devil, I'm not sure I could have continued. Efram had said – let's do it, but I decided a pep talk would be in order before we entered the 'lion's den'.

"When we get up there, we stay close together, understand?"

They both nodded.

"No matter what we witness, we are there serving God and preventing Drake releasing The Lord of the Underworld. We will all feel like turning around and dashing back down this tunnel, I realise that. So far, I have not been the strongest member of our trio......."

"I think over the past hour or so, you've made amends for that," said Peter. "If anything, it was me......."

"You have been incredible, Peter," I told him. "And so, have you, Efram. All I am saying is, together we are stronger." I put my arms around them. "Are you ready for the final battle?"

"As ready as I'll ever be," said Efram.

Peter nodded, swallowing hard. I wondered if my eyes mirrored his fear.

I began the climb, my legs feeling like lead, my stomach turning somersaults. I prayed to a God I'd never given a thought to before we moved to Chanter's Hide. For that, I felt a deep sense of remorse and guilt. I wasn't that full of my own importance not to realise that I was just a tool, someone in the right place at the right time. For the time being, God's will and mine were the same – to prevent untold evil being unleashed into this world. He was using me, and I was using him to save Jan and Charlie, it was as simple as that.

The darkness began to lift, and I knew we weren't far away from Drake's abominable temple. With the silvery glow came the stink of corruption. I had never thought about it before but, evil does reek. Nevertheless, I took in a deep breath. We rounded the final bend and the sound of debauchery was added to the mix. The fetid air was filled with chants and cries, increasing in intensity and expectation. The last fifty yards felt like we were dragging ourselves through a swamp. I don't know if that was our trepidation or some spell Drake had cast. I suspected the former. I reached behind me.

"Hold my hand, Efram. Peter, hold your Dad's hand. When we're in that hellhole, don't let go. Whatever happens, don't let go."

I took the final steps and lead us to the gates of hell.

It was a sea of blood red robes. The 'Hiders' were out in force. They were chanting and swaying, their glazed eyes fixed on their leader. Drake was in a black robe, with red symbols, inverted crosses, and pentagrams. On his head was a horned mask. Shona was beside him, swaying along with the others, her robe hanging loosely around her biceps, showing most of her breasts, her nipples hard against the velvet. In her hands was a black cushion, a silver ceremonial dagger resting on its surface. Jan and Hannah lay on the makeshift altar, covered by a red, satin sheet. I thanked God for small mercies, although. I knew it wouldn't be long before the sheet was thrown off. They appeared to be asleep. Again, I thanked God. At the front of the group was Hannah's husband, Nick. He moved along with the rest of the villagers, his mouth forming the weird phrases being chanted. It was obviously Latin but, apart from that, I didn't have a clue what was being said. Nick's eyes were not glued to the vicar, like the rest. His attention was on his wife and unborn child. He must have known what was about to happen and, by the look on his face, was dreading it. The poor chap had no chance of stopping the slaughter and, I'm sure, if he had tried, the rest of them would have ripped him limb from limb.

Efram and Peter followed me out of the tunnel, and we stood side by side watching Drake play to his crowd. He was in raptures, a pop idol on a stadium stage. If this ritual weren't so deadly serious, it would be laughable. Behind him the night air seemed to shimmer and every so often I caught a faint glimpse of a terrifying figure. The huge head of a goat, horns glistening with blood, steam pouring from savage nostrils, was atop the body of a massive male, its semi erect member swinging between its legs.

"The Goat of Mendes," I whispered. "The devil himself."

I could feel Efram and Peter shaking as they squeezed my hands.

"We must be strong," I said.

It was at that moment that Drake, enjoying the adoration, looked around his congregation and spotted us.

"Ah, we have guests." He waved a hand in our direction.

The crowd turned and wailed like banshees. They were about to move towards us.

"Leave them, my children. They will have a good view from there." He turned his attention back to us. "I must thank you, Ben, for bringing your wife and child to Chanter's Hide. It enabled me to bring the true Lord's re-emergence forward. Now, you can watch as they give their pitiful lives to assist in his rising. I believe your friends are wishing they'd changed allegiance."

Efram's grip tightened and I squeezed back.

"Go to hell," he said, through gritted teeth.

Peter took a step forward, looked to the sky and spoke in tongues. That is the only way I can describe it, I'm afraid. Drake tried to hide his concern but failed. He threw back the sheet covering Jan and Hannah and I gasped.

Both were naked, as I expected. Their bodies, in the full bloom of motherhood, were daubed in blood. For a split second, I thought we were too late, then, I saw the lamb's carcass at the side of the altar, its throat cut, the last of its life force merging with the dried blood of its predecessors. Drake looked at me, beckoning Shona forward. She used the cushion as an accessory for her 'whore's' dance. She pulled open her robe until her breasts were exposed. She moved her free hand downwards, thrusting her hips forward. Drake bent down and kissed her savagely, squeezing her breast with one hand and placing his other over hers as it slipped between her legs. All the time, his eyes never left mine. His smile widened as my disgust became more apparent. He pushed his 'bitch' to one side, grabbing the dagger from the cushion as she slid to the floor, reaching for his erection.

Efram and I glared at him. I could hear Efram grinding his teeth and, suddenly, realised I was doing the same. Peter was stock still, speaking softly in a language that was alien to me. It sounded Arabic or Yiddish. I couldn't help thinking that if this were a novel, the author would know exactly what was being said and in which tongue. Reality, in this case, did not mirror fiction.

Drake started to caress my wife's pregnant belly and I nearly lost it. The hurt, confusion, humiliation and anger raged through me. I bit my tongue, feeling the blood in my mouth.

"God, how much longer?"

Efram moved his hand from mine and thrust his arm around my waist. "I feel him," he said. "We'll know when it's time."

Drake raised the dagger in the air and my eyes were fixed on the blade. I could see the tiny, dried blood stains, the scratches where the knife had hit bone.

"Are we his children?" Drake screamed.

His 'flock' gave him an almighty 'Yes'.

Drake brought the knife down and my heart nearly burst from my chest. I saw the blood spurt over Jan and Hannah as the blade slashed Shona's throat. The surprise in her eyes quickly turned to realisation as her hands reached feebly to stem the flow. She was in the throes of death as Drake lifted his foot and kicked her to the ground.

"You see, Ben, we all have to make sacrifices. I've made mine. Are you ready to make yours?"

The 'Hiders' turned to us, their bloodlust ignited, their faces eager. I had never felt so much disgust.

"Have you forgotten the face of God?" I said.

I saw Nick's face. It was filled with fear but, now held a little hope. I could feel the air prickling around me. I looked back at Drake.

"Sacrifice is a necessity."

He lifted the knife again.

The atmosphere grew heavy and sulphurous, the night a commotion of emotion. Drake's followers became agitated. The vicar paused, the knife above his head. I could feel God's light burning into my soul, and I rejoiced.

Peter moved forward, arms outstretched, his hands shimmering.

At first, I was fearful of his breaking our trinity, but soon realised that we were now, all three, God's willing disciples. I let the light shine through my eyes into Drake's, watching as his uncertainty turned into panic. He let the hand holding the knife drop to his side. He wheeled around and grabbed Nick by the throat.

"My Lord needs more power," I heard him mutter. The knife came up and sliced through Nick's jugular vein, spraying more blood over Jan and Hannah.

The image behind Drake intensified, the face beneath the horns, scarred and heinous, a vision of true evil. The devil was a gossamer wing away from invading our world. The vicar hacked and yanked until he held Nick's severed head in his hand. His expression was manic. He hurled the head towards us.

"Behold the true Lord," he cried, lifting the knife above Jan's belly. I saw Charlie's foot push against the skin before all Heaven broke loose.

Peter grabbed his Father's hand. Efram was still digging his nails into mine.

"See your God and never forget his face," we said in unison, allowing His power to flow through us. Drake's Satanic temple was filled with a brilliance, a light so intense it burned the blood-stained rocks. The 'Hiders' cowered, falling to the ground in fear.

The three of us faced Drake and his 'Lord'. The Goat of Mendes twitched and squirmed, before fading. Drake, himself, was trying to bring the knife down and continue his obscene, sacrificial ceremony. His arm appeared to be frozen in mid-air.

He screamed as the light enveloped him, the flesh melting from his bones, the bones crumbling to dust. I screamed in righteous exhilaration. He was dead.

God's will had been done, His light withdrew from the tired rock, leaving it cleansed.

I ran over to Jan and Hannah, feeling a mixture of relief and despair. I threw the sheet back over both of them and hugged them. They were still in a drug induced sleep.

I looked at the shaking forms on the ground. Efram and Peter joined me.

"Do you now know your God?" I asked them.

It was Joe, the landlord of the 'Duck and Pheasant' who raised his head.

"Thank you," he said. "We have lived in fear for so long. He had ....power. He could make us do whatever he wanted."

"Spineless bunch of buggers," Efram said, under his breath.

"We envied your courage," said Sam Templeton. He looked back at me. "And your uncle Ted, too. When you arrived, we were hoping for a knight in shining armour. I guess our hopes became reality."

TWENTY-TWO

"D'you think you can say sorry, and everything will be fine?" Efram said, a disgusted sneer distorting his features. "You have all been complicit in every kind of evil, including the murder of innocent babies. He was just one man, there are over forty of you. You let him rule this village and bowed down to him, as if he were 'God'".

Sam Templeton's wife grabbed her husband's hand. "He's right, we deserve the same fate as him." She jerked a thumb in the direction of Drake's smoking remains.

"He paralysed me once," said Joe. "I'm a strong man and I stood up to him. No-one has ever pushed me around and I've never run away from a fight. I took a swing at him and my body froze. I had to watch whilst he raped my wife, unable to lift a finger. He held a dagger to her throat and asked if I wanted him to kill her. I couldn't even shake my head." The tears rolled down the big man's cheeks. "He released me and told me that if I ever challenged him again, it would be the last thing I did. I had never been so terrified."

Ena, the local shopkeeper stepped forward. "We were all terrified of him, we lived in fear for our lives. He gave you one warning and that was it, if you overstepped the mark again, you were dead. Your uncle Ted didn't heed his warning."

"Something we'll always be thankful for," said Sam. "If he had, you wouldn't have come to the village and nothing would have changed. I believe Ted knew the sacrifice he was making."

The sneer hadn't left Efram's face but, for myself, I felt for these people. If it hadn't been for Efram's and Peter's help, I could have been just like them. If we hadn't found the pieces to our puzzle, I wondered whether God would have helped us anyway. I liked to believe, he would.

"This is God's place now," I said. "All are welcome who wish to stay and live a good and peaceful life. If there are any among you who still wish to follow the dark path, you are no longer needed here."

Every single villager fell to his or her knees, hands in supplication.

Efram looked at me with a – do you know what you're doing – sort of expression.

I heard a murmur and looked over to Jan and Hannah. They were beginning to wake.

"I need a couple of those robes," I said to Joe.

He and Sam took off theirs, covering their nether regions with their hands.

"I don't know how I'm going to tell Hannah about Nick," I said to Efram.

"Do you want me to do it?"

I put my hand on his shoulder. "No, but thanks. I have to do this."

I walked over to the two women with a heavy heart. It is a fact – no battle ends without casualties.

I put the first robe around Hannah first. I needed to get her away from the headless body of her husband and to relative safety before whatever drug Drake had used on them wore off completely. I sat her up, holding the robe around her shoulders. I pulled it tight, covering her completely.

"Can you stand?" I asked softly.

She looked at me with glazed eyes and I repeated the question. "Hannah, can you stand?"

There appeared to be a glimmer of recognition before she nodded her head.

"I... I. think so, you're Ben, aren't you? Where are we?"

I lifted her gently from the altar, letting her lean her weight on my shoulders.

"Don't worry about that. We just need to get you home."

Efram had walked towards me. "Take care of your wife, Ben, "he said. "There's time for the other thing, when we're away from here."

I nodded and passed Hannah into his care. I heard him say 'Come on my dear, let's get you out of here, you'll be fine soon."

I wished that could be true. Hannah's pain hadn't begun yet. The villagers gave her space as she staggered at Efram's side, the look on all their faces one of terrible guilt and utter sorrow. She would have all the support we could give her, but that wouldn't bring Nick back.

I took Jan into my arms and put the robe around her. I couldn't stop the tears. "Are you okay, sweetheart?"

There was terror in her eyes. "He drugged me, Ben. You were right, "she said quietly, her own tears falling. "He took me to the vicarage, that's the last thing I remember. Where is he?" She started to look around wildly. I stepped between her and Nick's body. Unfortunately, she saw the dead lamb. She grimaced.

"He's gone," I said, "He won't bother us again. I'll explain it all later when we're home and you've had some rest."

"Hannah was there, as well," she said as I eased her to the ground. "Is she alright?"

"She's fine," I said. "Efram's taking care of her."

Efram was right, telling them both about Nick's death would wait, especially for Jan. His absence would have to be explained to Hannah much sooner, regrettably.

Peter came over to us, his limp gone altogether. "Hello Mrs. Ebbrell, I'm Peter." He held out his hand.

Jan managed a sickly smile. "Pleased to meet you, Peter. Ben has told me about you and your Dad. I believe you've become good friends."

"The best. Your husband's a hero, Mrs. Ebbrell, a real hero."

I put my other arm around him. "There are no heroes here, Peter. Just normal people who can now, live a normal life. Now, let's get off this rock."

It didn't seem to take anywhere near the amount of time to make our way back to where we'd moored our dinghy, as it had to reach Drake's lair. The villagers followed us. There were now a dozen or more rowing boats there as well.

Efram was already helping Hannah into one of the larger ones.

"I'm sure no-one will mind if we take this boat," he said sharply.

"No, no, take it by all means," said Sam Templeton. "It's my boat – it's the least I can do."

Efram glared at him. I could see he was about to subject the farmer to a verbal assault. I caught his eye and shook my head.

"Recriminations are not going to get us anywhere, my friend."

Efram was in mental and emotional turmoil, that was clear. All through Drake's reign of terror, he'd stood his ground and distanced himself from the vicar's regime. The fact that Drake had allowed him to do that was a key factor though.

If he had suffered a similar fate to Joe, I wondered if he would have been so stoic. If Drake had rendered him powerless and threatened to do his worst with Peter, I doubt he would have been so pious. We will all do everything we can to protect our loved ones, and that is exactly what the inhabitants of Chanter's Hide had done.

Peter and I helped Jan into the boat and, as Efram picked up the oars, Joe stepped forward, an old sack covering his modesty.

"We thank God for sending you to us," he said. He looked around the rest of the villagers. "We all do."

They all bowed their heads, muttering – 'Thank God' or 'Praise the Lord'.

"We will meet in the pub tomorrow morning at ten o'clock," I said. "It's time for a new beginning. In the meantime, we all need some rest. Go home and sleep."

"I don't know if I'll ever sleep again," said Joe. "After all I've done and seen."

I stood at the side of the boat. "Listen to me, all of you. Without God's help, Efram, Peter and I would have been there with you, participating in Drake's atrocities. My uncle Ted led the way, we just followed. As a village, we will put this behind us and make Chanter's Hide a place to be happy and proud to live in.

I realise it won't be easy but, with God on our side, we will come through it.

Now, I need to get my wife and Hannah home. We'll see you in the morning."

I pushed the boat into the water, jumped in and Efram began to row. I pulled Jan close to me.

"I'm so sorry," she said.

"What for?"

"For not believing you."

"There's nothing to be sorry for, sweetheart, he was very convincing and very charming, and it must have seemed like I was losing the plot. It's how he planned it, believe me. He delighted in tormenting me, revealing his plans for you and Hannah, knowing you would never believe them. He was, after all, the local vicar."

Hannah shivered at my other side.

"Are you cold Hannah?"

Her voice was small and childlike. "Where's Nick? Where's my husband?"

I looked behind at Efram. His shrug said – it's up to you. I couldn't tell Hannah a lie and I couldn't ignore her question. I had hoped the drug would have lasted a little longer and I could have managed to get her to sleep for a few hours before I had to give her the terrible news.

"I am so sorry," I said. "He's with God now."

She looked at me, her eyes wide and shook her head. "No," she said, shaking her head violently. "No. You must take me to him, he'll be worried."

I put my arm around her, and she pulled away.

"Don't do that, Nick won't like it. He's very possessive, you know."

Efram leant forward. "I'm sorry my love, but Ben's telling you the truth. Your husband died helping to save you and your child."

I thanked him mentally for his speed of thought. His statement wouldn't lessen Hannah's grief but, as the time passed, her husband would be a hero to her and their child. My arm was still outstretched, and I just managed to catch her as she fell back in a dead faint.

"Thanks, Efram," I said. "That will mean everything to her in the future."

"Nick is dead?" Jan said quietly.

"I'm afraid so darling, Drake killed him just before we could save you."

"What did Nick do?"

I didn't lie. "He lost his life for his wife and unborn child. That's all any man could do."

"How terrible. Poor Hannah. We must do all we can to help her, Ben."

"Don't worry, the whole village will rally round."

"I thought you hated the 'Hiders'?"

"I did, until I learned the truth. They were all under Drake's sadistic spell, terrified for their lives. If it hadn't been for these two," I jerked a thumb over my shoulder. "That could have been me, as well."

Hannah began to stir. I had wished she would have been out for a little longer.

She opened her eyes and stared straight ahead. "I can't go back to that house," she said softly.

"You're coming home with us," said Jan, before I could open my mouth. "You'll stay as long as you want to, for good, if you wish."

"Our home is yours," I said.

The beach was about a hundred yards away and Efram eased off on the oars. After a few seconds, Peter leapt into the shallow water and pulled the boat onto the sand. He was like a different lad, strong and confident, his affliction gone completely. He had served his God and had been rewarded. I turned to Efram and saw the tears in his eyes.

"I love that boy," he said.

Gradually the rest of the villagers came ashore. I looked over to where Chanter House was in full flame, being cleansed by righteous fire. Joe came to my side.

"That's a sight for sore eyes, "he said. "Thank you, from the bottom of my heart, Ben. You have saved us all."

I clapped him on the back. "All down to the big man," I said, pointing upward.

"Maybe so, but he still needed to find the right men for the job."

"Well, whatever, tomorrow is a new day and a new start for Chanter's Hide. In time Drake and his whore will be a distant, if horrible, memory. Now, we all need to do whatever we can for Hannah. She lost the love of her life tonight."

He nodded. "Nick was a good lad, we'll all miss him, and we'll all be there for Hannah. Don't you worry about that."

"Jan and I are taking to ours tonight. We have a spare room and she's welcome to use it for as long as she wants to. One saving grace – he didn't manage to take her baby away from her."

"I'm so sorry Ben, we should have done............"

"Joe," I said, cutting his apology short. "There were only two people responsible for all of the evil that happened in this place, and they're both gone. Go home and get some rest. I'll see you in the morning."

I left him staring at the inferno that was Chanter House. In the morning there would be little left of it, just a mass of rubble. I re-joined Jan, Hannah, Efram and Peter. Efram had his arm around his son.

"Do you really think this village can survive all that has happened?" Efram asked me.

"The evil that was here, my friend, has been eradicated. If we all pull together, this will be a place where everyone is proud and happy to be. The thing we mustn't do is to blame people for being terrified of a powerful man, a servant of the devil. I know it took every ounce of my strength to do what we did, and we had God helping us. I think that goes for all three of us, don't you?"

He sighed. "I'm not afraid to admit it – there were a few times I nearly soiled my underwear. I suppose, after Drake had gone, I just saw red. I remembered the way they used to look at Peter and I."

"I think that was Drake's biggest mistake. He looked upon you two as pathetic misfits and enjoyed the ostracism you were subjected to. He never believed you could become a threat. In a way, he was a victim of his own ego."

"Will you be okay with Hannah? We have room at our place, you know."

"Thanks, Efram but I think she needs Jan at the moment. I think, in time, they'll be more like sisters, rather than friends. I don't expect any of us to get much in the way of sleep tonight, especially Hannah. I'll see you in the morning, my friend."

AFTER

Chanter's Hide is well into its summer months and it promises to be a scorcher. Ten months have passed since that terrible night. It was a long, cold, wet winter but the villagers were united in their desire to make the village a haven for all. Jan gave birth to Charlotte on the ninth of September, Hannah following close behind on the fourteenth. She named her son Nicholas, for obvious reasons. She stayed with us for six months after the murder of her husband and Jan and I did our best to help her through the dark times. She will never forget Nick, especially as Nick junior is the spit of him. I think that helps. During the time she was with us, the villagers gave her cottage a real makeover. Even so, we never mentioned to her about moving back in, that had to be her decision. As I had thought, she and Jan have become the best of friends, bordering on sisters.

The site where Chanter House stood has been cleared but no matter how hard we try to turn it into a memorial garden for the poor souls destroyed by Drake, nothing will grow there. At present, Joe is heading a team to concrete over the entire site and put benches and potted plants there. Evil will never win again in Chanter's Hide.

I have finished my first novel and it has been taken by an agent in Oxford who tells me he has two publishers interested. In the meantime, I make a living from proof reading. We are still pretty much self-efficient in the village but, at least, we can now leave if we fancy going into Bridport for a meal or just a trip out.

There is also real money in the village now. The production of meat, fruit and veg has increased and is being sold to independent traders throughout the county. Joe's wonderful ales are becoming popular with the landlords of free houses in the area. There is still a bartering system for those that want to carry on in that vein and I think there always will be. Quite a few of the younger members of our throng have jobs in Bridport or Dorchester. At the last count we had six more pregnancies in the village, a cause for rejoicing rather than fear and trepidation. Chanter's Hide is a happy place where everyone looks out for each other. I doubt if a more close-knit community could be found anywhere in the world.

We even have broadband now. A group of us contacted Virgin Media and arranged to dig in and lay fibre optic cable across the fields to the nearest connection box in Burton Bradstock. We even laid the cables in the village itself. We have one account for everyone, and no-one is ever late paying their dues. Even mobile phones work in the village now, as long as they are connected to EE. We get tourists passing through and a few have stayed at the pub, where Joe and Kathy are now offering bed and breakfast. Sam Templeton is thinking about turning one of his barns into a couple of holiday lets. It would be nice to welcome strangers to our little slice of paradise. The only thing we're missing is a school but, as the one at Burton is less than two miles away, that's not really a problem.

Smugglers' Rock is now a haven for gulls, and someone has spotted a couple of puffins there. It seems the place has been well and truly cleansed.

Efram and Peter are regular dinner guests and we get together for a spot of fishing, an activity I never dreamed of liking but now love. Peter is in the best of health and has found he has a knack for painting and decorating. Already some of the villagers have regaled themselves of his services. In a couple of years, he will be eighteen and I am sure he'll ply his trade across the county. I think I can speak for Jan when I say that this is the happiest either of us has ever been. I pulled down the old shed in the back garden and Efram and Peter helped me erect a small summer house, which I use for my work. We are now a real family with real friends, living in a place we love. Charlie is a spirited, young lady and is always making us laugh with her antics. She will most definitely be a tomboy. We love her dearly. Jan has just appeared in the doorway with Charlie in her arms, wearing her bathing costume and sun hat, looking as gorgeous as ever. It would appear, we are going to the beach.

THE END

Printed in Poland
by Amazon Fulfillment
Poland Sp. z o.o., Wrocław